Things Changed

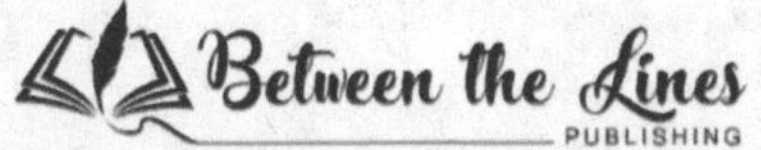

Willow River Press is an imprint of Between the Lines Publishing. The Willow River Press name and logo are trademarks of Between the Lines Publishing.

Between the Lines Publishing
1769 Lexington Avenue N, Ste 286
Roseville MN 55113
btwnthelines.com

Published November 2022
ISBN: (Paperback) 978-1-958901-05-2
ISBN: (Ebook) 978-1-958901-06-9

Things Changed

Patrick Jones

1 / Johanna

"Johanna, it's Paul."

I earned an A in AP Physics as a high school senior, so I know time can't stand still, but hearing Paul's voice again makes me question that. It makes me question everything.

"Johanna, it's Paul," he repeats."

This is the phone call I've been dreading; this is the call I've been craving. In an instant, I am thrust from a successful, first-year Columbia University student back to my insecure Pontiac, Michigan, high school self. All it took was this voice from my past.

"Hello. You remember me, right?" he says, then laughs. It is a sound I have missed.

I know his laugh is quicksand, but I can't resist.

"Paul, of course I remember you. I'm just surprised to hear from you, that's all."

"It's been a while, Joha, hasn't it?" I tingle at the use of his nickname for me.

"Yes, you could say that," I say, instead of the real answer, which is, *'No, Paul it's not been a while. It's been over two years since we talked.'* Other than visiting me at my high school graduation open house, mainly to show off his new girlfriend, Sarah, Paul had been out of my life. No calls, no texts, no messages. The past was in the past, but now things had changed.

"I need to ask a favor," he says. I wonder if he remembers not the last time we spoke, but the first. I said, *'I want you to kiss me,'* never knowing how those six words would be the dividing line of my life. Over two years later and I still exist on before and after Paul time.

"I'm sorry about this crappy cell-phone connection. It runs hot and cold, a lot like the Bird's engine these days."

The Bird. His black Firebird. The place we came together; the place we broke apart.

"Sorry, I'm just a little—" I start, then stop. I don't know what I am. Happy? Sad? I'm running hot and cold myself. Paul did that to me; there was never an in-between.

"If you can't help me, I get it; it's been a while. I just don't know who else to turn to," he says, each word softer than the last like it's getting harder to say the words asking for help. "You were always there for me before, so can you help now?"

I put my foot in the quicksand. "What do you need?" I hold my breath and do the math: 25% of me wants him to say *'I need you, Johanna,'* but the other 75% is stronger, wiser, and more mature. There is knowing and there is knowing better; it was a line I never quite understood when I was with Paul. The fact I answer him this way shows I've learned nothing in a year at an Ivy League university. I'm sucked back into Pontiac West High drama with just one call.

"I just need a ride. That's all I need, Joha."

"Is the Bird dead?"

"I lost my license. I need a ride, please. It's important." He sounds stressed out.

"When? Where?"

"Here. Now."

I laugh out of a muscular memory because laughing is what I did most when I was with Paul. When I wasn't with him, I remember mostly crying bitter tasting tears.

"You got some wheels, Joha?"

"I'm driving my mom's car while I'm home for the summer." I know he can't see me over the phone, but I'm staring at my bedroom floor, embarrassed. I'm nineteen with a year at Columbia University under me, yet still borrowing mom's car like some high school kid.

"Not that big white Jeep with the dented fender she used to drive?"

"The same one," I answer. How does he remember details about my mom's car?

"Let's be like the Boss. Let's be born to run!" My memory is an Ipod shuffle as the Bruce Springsteen catalog flips through my brain.

"Are you still living in your mom's trailer?" I ask, then hate myself for doing so.

He doesn't answer with words, just a loud growl like a caged animal, but then he starts singing the first few lines of "Thunder Road" and I join in out of habit, out of memory. We sing Springsteen together, our voices as one, just like we did before things changed between us forever.

"Where do you think you're going?" mom asks. She is dressed for work even though she lost her high-pressure job at Chrysler. My dad's still working but for how much longer? Afraid of losing his job, he's working longer hours. He's never home, and I miss him.

"I'm going out," I announce.

"Don't you start your job today?" Mom still mass-produces questions, another one always coming down the assembly line unlike the idle factories in most of Michigan.

"Tomorrow." I'm working at the Barnes & Noble at The Villages of Rochester Hills.

"Then where are you going so early?"

"Out." This is the tone of talk with mom since my junior year. This high school honor student sounds like a third grader in the face of her mother's inquiry onslaught. The less I say, the less there is for us to argue about, which is all it seems we've done for two plus years.

"Don't forget that I need my car later today," she reminds me.

"Why?" I know why, but I sadly admit to the joy in twisting the knife.

"I have a job interview."

I swallow a smile and a sneer. "Another one?" Another twist.

Mom lights up a smoke and walks into the kitchen. She pours herself a cup of coffee. My cup is next to the pot, but she doesn't fill it. I fill up the Columbia travel mug, grab the keys, and head out the door. I leave my mom behind knowing I will soon be next to Paul again.

I honk and then wait in the car for Paul. The honking sound adds to the sound stew of the trailer park. I'm afraid to knock on his door, afraid to see his mother. In the nine months Paul and I were together, I think I only met her two or three times. Paul and I arranged our time so we'd never see her, mostly by visiting his trailer Wednesday nights while she was at church. I wasn't just visiting Paul, we were also "visiting the grandparents" as Paul called us having sex because the first time we hooked up was in my grandparent's house. Doing it at his trailer when his mom was gone, I figured out later, wasn't just about opportunity, but the motive of Paul's anger toward her. Only Paul could make something beautiful as sex also an ugly act of rage.

But that was my relationship with Paul: beautiful and ugly. Beautiful like the red roses he brought me every payday; ugly like the black and blue marks he left all over my body.

I click open the door lock when he arrives. Other than the faded blue suit rather than jeans and a Springsteen tee, from his long stringy blonde hair down to his beat-up black

Chucks, he looks exactly the same. It's the same face I've seen in my dreams and my nightmares, in my regrets and in my aspirations. It's the unshaven face that rubs against my life and leaves a mark.

"Thanks, I owe you, Joha," he says as he climbs in the car. He doesn't try to kiss me.

"Where to?" I ask as I pull away from his trailer. His Firebird sits on the street in front of the trailer. I gaze around the surroundings and see older and more beat-up, probably abandoned, cars parked in front or up on blocks by the side. It's like an auto cemetery.

"You like nice," he says. Liar. Despite spending a school year in NYC, the fashion capital of the country, I don't think I learned anything. I'm still a clothes klutz. A blue Columbia t-shirt, a denim jacket, and Target jeans don't equal nice. Just normal, boring, like me.

"Thanks," I mumble. I never learned how to take a compliment that well since they were few and far between in my house, except when it came to earning an academic honor.

"How was Columbia?" Before I can answer, he says. "Turn right toward the expressway." Like daddy's good little Marine girl that I once was, I'm still good at following orders. I gently push the gas. After nine months in New York, I'm not used to driving again.

"Okay," I answer. Paul reduces me to sounding stupid like I forgot how to talk.

"So, Columbia?" I don't know if he wants to hear my story or just listen to my voice.

"Fun, scary, difficult."

"Sounds like me." He lets out a small laugh. I explode with a bigger one.

I feel the need to put up a barrier before Paul tries to cross a closed bridge. "I met a really nice guy, Roman, so mostly fun I guess," I lie. When I met Roman, he was nice, he was fun, but that changed when he got clinging and controlling just like Paul used to be. Why does everything sweet leave me with a bitter taste? Roman cheated on me like Paul, except with Roman it was another woman, while with Paul, it was a six-pack of beer and a stash of secrets.

"'Roman'? Did he lend you his ear? Was he epileptic and had a lot of Caesars? Did —"

"Where are we going?" I interrupt to stop the pun fest.

"Head south on 75, toward downtown," he answers.

I feel like I missed a bullet. Wasn't where we are going asked and answered? We're going nowhere. We're gone. We're done. I told him the night we broke-up, "*Paul, you are part of my past, not part of my future.*" Why am I here? I ask myself all these questions, yet still I drive on out of habit and more than mild curiosity. I always wondered what happened to his life after I ended things between us.

"I'd like to know where we're going," I say as I carefully merge onto the expressway.

"A little place called 'You'll See,'" he says. "Can I have some Joe, Joha?"

Before I can answer, he grabs the coffee mug, takes a sip from it, and then pretends like he's going to spit it out. "Too sweet. What are you, a twelve-year-old girl?"

"That's how I like it." I feel embarrassed when I say it.

"You see, you leave Pontiac for New York, and it changes you," he says. "You're from Michigan. We drink our coffee black, drive our cars fast, and export our jobs to Mexico."

"My mom lost her job." I keep my eyes on the road and the focus off me.

"Well, at least she had a job unlike my lazy mom," Paul says showing his usual disdain for his mom. I remember their screaming matches at his front porch like they happened yesterday.

I steal a glance. He looks at the floor like it contains some answers. "My mom hasn't worked in years, not since my dad," Paul says, cutting his sentence short.

I flinch. Another muscle memory. Any mention of his dad was Paul's anger trigger. The worst time he beat me down—what should've been the last time, but it wasn't—was because I mentioned the father that abandoned him. The dad that Paul wouldn't let go. From driving the same car to listening to Springsteen because that was his dad's music, Paul kept his dead father very much alive.

"But I'm working. Saving money to move out to Cali and live with Brad."

"That's great," I say, but it is the opposite of how I feel. Every now and then, I call or text Brad who was Paul's best friend in high school who I think understood Paul more than I ever could. At first, I stayed in touch with Brad to learn about Paul, but over time, Brad and I developed a friendship based on being Pontiac public school kids at elite universities, me at Columbia and him at Stanford. I knew from Brad that he and Paul were not in touch. If Paul is planning on moving there, then Brad knows nothing about it. I know that Paul's lying, again. He lied about so much, yet until the very end, I chose to believe him.

"Okay, next exit," he says. He now sounds calm and relaxed, a much different tone than I remember, which was normally whiplashing between a whisper and a shout. Near the end of our time together, it was nothing but one long scream when we came apart in the torrent of his lies.

I fake a half smile, thinking how the 25% of me who thought this was a good idea to see Paul again was 100% wrong. We drive mostly in silence except when he gives directions. As we exit, he tries to make jokes, but I'm barely listening. I believe nothing he says.

"Turn left into the parking lot." I obey. "Joha, can you come inside with me?"

"Inside?" I ask as I turn the corner and see the Oakland County Courthouse sign.

I sit in silence with Paul outside of a courtroom until a middle-aged man with little hair and less fashion sense than even me approaches us. The guy clicks on a fake smile like a switch.

"Paul, we need to talk," the guy says.

"About what?" Paul snaps.

"Your plea."

"Plea?" Paul sounds like someone smacked him in the face.

"Allison changed her mind. She said she would testify against you, so you have to take this plea," the guy—I assume Paul's lawyer—says. So much for privileged conversations. Paul answers by standing, then giving the wall a stiff kick. I'm in full question mode. What plea? Who is Allison? But the biggest question: What was I thinking?

"I knew she was a lying bitch."

My lips curl at the disrespectful word that spit out of Paul's mouth.

"If you plead, I can get you off without jail time since it is your first offense like this, and it is nothing big, just for making what the court calls terroristic threats. I doubt you'll do time."

Paul kicks the wall again, looks at me, and then another kick. This anger seems all too familiar. I snap back to the Valentine's Day dance. The strikes started as kicks against the dumpster in the bitter cold that left me with frozen tears of fear. By the end of that night, those kicks became slaps and a punch against my face. "I can't go to jail, again!" Paul shouts.

Like that punch, the word "again" causes my head to recoil.

Paul whispers something to the lawyer, who nods in response, then walks away.

"Paul, what have you gotten yourself into?" I whisper. I feel ashamed to be with him.

"It's a misunderstanding, but if she gets married, she will be Mrs. Understanding."

"I'm serious." My voice still quivers when I confront him.

"You were always too serious, Joha," he says. "It's a good thing you gave me a ride so you laughed for a while. I'm sure funny is Greek to Roman."

I stare at the ugly, pitted floor and think about those uglier words: "terroristic threats."

"Paul!" The lawyer shouts. He stands by the bathroom ten feet away.

"I gotta talk to this tool," Paul says. "Please wait for me."

Again, the Bruce catalog shuffles, and the words to *If I Should Fall Behind* fall on me. It was our song. It was the song we danced to at his senior prom; the song he played the morning we got back together after the Valentine's dance massacre. It was the song that fulfilled every immature notion I had about mature love. The idea of the song is people make mistakes, but you forgive. If your lover stumbles, you wait for them. But Paul didn't stumble; he struck me, but now he speaks like someone falling and in pain.

"Joha, please, wait for me, and I'll explain everything." In Paul's world, explanations equal excuses.

"I don't think this—"

Before I can finish, he hugs me like he's trying to pull me into his body. He kisses me on the cheek, and the stubble from his face tickles my skin. "Don't leave me behind again."

The word 'again' is another dagger yet trying to remove it from my heart is harder than I would have imagined. I take a deep breath like I was diving into the deep end of the pool.

From my seat outside of the courtroom, I people-watch. Like students on the day of a final exam, stress lines every forehead in this setting. I pull out my phone, push the number, and wait for my new best friend and fellow Columbia student, Sydney, to pick-up.

"Yo, Jo," she answers. As always, she's upbeat no matter the hour of the day or night.

"What's up?" I ask in desperate need of distracting conversation.

"My weight. A week back home, and I've already gained five pounds," she cracks. "I've eaten more in the last day than I did our last week at school. Damn you, Pontiac portions!"

I laugh, which encourages her to riff for another five minutes about our hometown. While I went to Pontiac West, Sydney went to East. We lived most of our lives less than twenty miles from each other but had to move to New York to find each other. We met during freshman orientation, found out we were from the same hometown, and started talking. It was a continuous conversation interrupted by sleep, studying, and seriously flawed freshman romances. Mine with Roman, a grad student from Canada; hers with Gan, a Thai student. With our international adventures ending in failure, we're back in

Michigan with only each other to lean on. Good thing she's added five more pounds because I'll need all the support she can offer now that I've let Paul squirm back into my life if only for one hour, which is one more than he deserves.

"Yo, Jo, you there?" she asks.

"Sorry, mind vacation," I answer. "What are you doing later?"

"Later? Latte. You, me, I see it in our future."

"Good, because I got something to tell you."

"Did you write the great American novel without me? I told you that I—"

"I saw Paul." Sydney knows everything about Paul. She knows about all the good times and all of the bad times that cancelled them out. All it took was one late night, way too much weed, and too many pent-up secrets for her to peer into my ugly past. "Don't hate me."

"I don't judge," she says, and I laugh, earning more than one dirty look for the stressed-out courthouse crowd. "What's so funny?"

"Just that you said judge," I reply. "I'm at the Oakland County Courthouse."

"Oh my God, you didn't marry him, did you?"

I laugh again, loud enough to gather yet more angry stares. I look up. Paul and his lawyer have vanished, like my common sense. "No. I didn't marry him."

"Then why?"

"Later, over latte."

"I gotta go anyway. I got to get to my part-time job at the National Coney Island. Just what I need, right? To be around food all day. Temptation is my full-time curse."

"I expect a best friend discount."

"And I expect best friend details about this Paul situation."

"It's a deal," she says. "Hey, did you start that book yet?"

I look in my purse at the paperback copy of *Howl* by Allen Ginsburg that she gave me. I still prefer thick fantasy novels, but Sydney insisted I read this book of poetry.

"It is the poem that started the beat movement. Besides, Ginsburg went to Columbia, and you have to read something by the second greatest poet who attended Columbia."

"Second? Who's the first?"

"You're talking to her now," Sydney says, then laughs. "I gotta go."

The phone clicks, and my eyes scan the hall again for Paul, but he's not there. I shake my head, frustrated more with me more than him. I open *Howl*, and I want to live the title. I want to scream to cleanse myself of all the confusion clogging my mind.

I keep reading the book when I notice something strange. On the other side of the courtroom waiting area is a guy who looks about my age. He's sitting with a middle-aged man, but he's looking at me. He's dressed for non-success with a goofy thrift store style get-up coupled with a tinted green ponytail. Like most people waiting, he doesn't look happy to be here.

I try to focus on the book, but he keeps peeking over at me, although not in a scary stalker way. He's not looking at his phone or the man sitting next to him; all his attention seems focused on me. I'm unnerved and flattered at the same time. I hide behind the pages of *Howl* and wait for Paul to return so I can get him home to get myself out of this situation I never should have gotten myself into in the first place. I sigh with exasperation and frustration at myself, but it is not the only sound I hear. I hear the guy sitting across the hallway speaking to me.

2 / *Bret*

"'So, how do you like the book?'" I ask the pretty girl with the short brown hair and big glasses sitting across from me.

She looks up confused as she seeks out the location of the phantom voice speaking to her. I get up from the hard chair and walk toward her. My green eyes peer from behind small granny glasses. The glasses are new. Everything else comes by way of my Goodwill employee discount.

"Did you say something to me?" the girl asks when I get closer.

"Nice shoes," I say, then tap my left foot in front of hers. Like me, she's wearing high-top Chucks, although she's got the classic black and white, while I'm flashing green to match my hair.

"You, too." She sees my shoes, laughs, then puts down her book to make eye contact.

"You know that book *Howl* started the whole Beat poetry movement," I say, then touch the top of the book.

"How do you know that?"

"I know lots of stuff," I say, then smile, which I hope hides how nervous I am. Talking to girls isn't a subject taught at University of Michigan-Flint, so I channel my probably former best friend, Alex, who chatted up many a waitress back in our Southwestern High School days.

"The one important thing I don't know is your name. My name's Bret, like the writer, Bret Harte, or retired wrestler, Bret Hart. It depends if you prefer sonnets or suplexes."

"Would a poetry slam be both?" she asks.

I laugh, then she smiles bright enough to light up the dim hallway filled with troubled souls.

"Maybe your name is anonymous," I ask.

She pauses like she's wondering why this weird lanky guy is bothering her. "Johanna."

I breathe a sigh of relief that I've gotten this far, so I decide to take another small step. "I got visions of Johanna."

"That's the title of a Bob Dylan song, right?" Pretty and smart is a sexy pairing.

"Want me to sing it for you?" I ask.

She doesn't really react, so I decide it is time to bring out the heavy material. "I was the lead singer in my band." I wonder if she sees my wince at the use of the past tense. Once Alex went to pursue his musical dreams in New York, our band Radio Free Flint died without him.

"Well, Bret you are a singer, scholar, and wrestling fan. You're a real Renaissance man."

Before I can say anything else, I hear my dad yell at me from down the hall. I turn around, shake my head, and sigh like my chest hurts. "Bret Hendricks. I live in deserted Flint and overpopulated Twitter, but I'm easy to find." I motion for her to hand me her book. She complies, and I take out my always handy Sharpie and writes a phone number and Twitter handle on the inside cover. "Check out videos of my band Radio Free Flint on YouTube. If you're in Flint, say hello to me at Goodwill East. Wait, no one ever chooses to be in Flint."

"It's not like Pontiac is that great."

"Compared to Flint, wait, I don't think anything compares to Flint, and I mean that in the worst way." With continued high unemployment and higher crime, my hometown is dying.

"So maybe I'll hear from you." I try to strike a tone of hopeful, not helpless or desperate.

She says nothing but does something much better, she raises her right eyebrow in a sign of friendly skepticism. I notice she's looking at me with a strange intensity and interest, which is good, especially since I expect rejection from most females since Becca in my senior year.

"Bret!" I feel a heavy hand on my skinny shoulder.

I turn around to see dad with his blood-shot eyes and whiskey breath. I am embarrassed as all hell. I leave Johanna, and I walk with dad down the ugly hallway. He seems to be making a beeline for the bathroom. I do what I resisted doing for so long, I follow him.

"Dad, what the hell is wrong with you?" I throw down while he throws up into the toilet. He's hung over on the morning he's facing a list of charges related to an accident he caused while driving drunk. I feel a little like throwing up myself being so bold with Johanna. I can talk the talk, but my knees shake at the thought of walking it. I long for human connection again but lack the skills and confidence to achieve it.

"Don't tell your mother about me being sick," he says. He's about to plead guilty on the advice of his lawyer, whom he hates. But then again, dad hates all lawyers.

"I'm going back to AA if I don't have to do time," dad says as he emerges from the stall. He's wearing a suit that doesn't fit. The last time I saw him in this suit was that morning at school in my junior year. It was the last time I saw him with a lawyer. It was also the last time we were really close when he saved my high school career by making a huge sacrifice for me.

"I'll drive you." I force back the laughter inside me as I recall how Dad refused to let me drive my mom's Chevy Metro until I showed him how to change the oil. I know he didn't really care about my changing the oil. It was just his way of getting me to do things his way, the hard way, the only way.

He washes his face in the sink, then looks in the mirror. I can tell he's wondering how his life fell apart so fast. It's a question that has no easy answer, but one root cause:

alcohol. Did he start drinking again and lose his job because of that, or once he lost his job, did he resume drinking? Did he start drinking once he sold his beloved Camaro to save our house and felt severed from this past? I ask these questions because my dad warned me off the big one: why?

"I'd better go face the music," he says. His gruff voice sounds a hundred years old.

In high school, he never attended my plays or listened to my music. Just like now, he hasn't gone to the few plays I've been in at the University of Michigan-Flint. Our long war ended two years ago during my junior year. We're not enemies but still by no means allies. Sometimes, I think the war isn't over; it's a cease fire waiting for the next spark to start our guns blazing.

"I gotta go find that bloodsucker." Dad wipes his face with a sandpaper quality brown paper towel and starts toward the door. "Thanks for coming, son."

"Of course," is all I can say, always a little stunned when he calls me 'son.'

He leaves the bathroom, but I stay behind. It's my turn to look at the man in the mirror, and like my dad, I'm not sure I like what I see. I wonder what this pretty and smart Johanna would see in someone like me. Only one person really saw me, and she hovers over me like a threatening storm cloud.

Kylee Edmonds.

She betrayed me, she broke my heart, and betrayed me again. I forgave her, yet I can't forget her. She used to call her overbearing, overly successful mother the

Shadowcaster, but Kylee plays that role in my life. All of my relationships ruined by her shadow. From Becca Levy in my high school senior year through a series of short-lived romances with theater girls during my college freshman year, I can't seem to get it right after being treated so wrong. Or did I have it so good that nothing can compare to Kylee? It's because of her—her dad, actually—that I know old Dylan songs like "Visions of Johanna." With this girl Johanna, maybe there's a chance. I recall telling Alex that guys who are fives don't get girls who are tens since I understood the awful arithmetic of animal attraction. This girl's a safe seven. She doesn't have Kylee's beauty or perfect dancer's body, then again, few do. But if she's reading *Howl*, she's got some smarts and hipness even without rainbow ribbons in her hair and piercings in her nose like Kylee sported this morning in the picture I saw of her on Instagram. Kylee's gone from Michigan, but she's got a handcuff on my heart, or maybe she's an addiction. Maybe I need Kylee Edmunds like dad needs cheap whiskey.

I walk with dad and the lawyer into the courtroom. Even though we live in Flint, dad found a temp factory job in Pontiac, and that's where he smashed into another car driving while he was drunk. For once, he was lucky as nobody got seriously hurt, except for dad's life. I know from what he said that it is about to change for the worse if the judge decides he has to trade in his blue coveralls for an orange County-issued uniform.

I sit in the back row since I don't need to hear any of this. I don't want to see any of this. I never saw dad seem so small before. His drinking days were over, he said, on the day I was born, but he broke that promise to himself. I know all about breaking promises to myself when I swore I'd never get back with Kylee, but I was in her arms—then her bed—the first chance I got after she cheated on me with my friend and bandmate Sean.

It doesn't take long. A hundred days in jail, a hefty fine, which he can't pay, and they suspend his license for a year, which means when he gets out, I'll be his chauffeur service, driving him around in the Metro since his Camaro no longer takes center stage in our garage. He sold it the first time to afford a lawyer to save my high school hide, then bought it back with the money we made off the settlement the lawyer won in the civil suit from when Dave Hitchings beat me up at prom. But then he lost it a second time to save the house. He told me once it reminded him of when he had the life he always wanted. I hate to admit, but I'm like my dad in that way. Those YouTube videos of Radio Free Flint reminds me of the best time I've had in my short nineteen years on this spinning sphere. I was in front singing, Alex was thrashing madly, Sean was laying down a funk punk beat, and by the stage dancing was Kylee.

Now she's in upstate New York, going to Vassar while I'm stuck in Flint with an alcoholic father who stomps his way toward me. "Let's go!" Dad shouts. During my junior year, I learned that the nail that sticks out the farthest gets hammered the hardest. I thought Dave Hitchings, dad, and school were the hammers, but I was wrong. Kylee was the hammer; I was the nail. and two years later, whenever I think about her—which is every day—I feel beaten down and bent permanently out of shape.

3 / *Johanna*

"Star, I need a ride again." It is Paul on the phone again, which could have been expected. He has been calling and texting me since last week when I took him to court.

My heart jumps a beat when he uses this other old nickname for me because he told me I was the bright star in his dark night life. He gave me, or maybe branded me, with a star necklace I still wear to this day as a memento of our good times together. I know better than to answer his call, but I can't turn him away again.

"It's important. I need to get to my court-ordered anger management class," Paul says.

I want to tell him it would have been nice if he would have attended this before we went out.

"You there, Star?" He asks, his voice is rough like he hasn't been sleeping, but mostly, I wonder if he's been drinking. Alcohol often fueled his flame of anger directed toward me.

I still don't answer. Am I there for him after two years or are the scars still too fresh?

"I really need your help, Star." He keeps using that name to capture me in his web.

"I can't really continue to—"

"I mean, you want me to get better, don't you?"

He's put me between the rock and the hard place. How can I answer no? "Of course."

"This is going to change everything."

I pause again. Paul had chances to change before and never did. Why should I think, being a few years older would make a difference? Could people like Paul even change? Could I? The fact I was talking with him again and doing what he asked makes me question myself.

"Star, are you there?" He asks again, trying to jolt me from my silence, which is just disguised self-reflection. "I guess I could hitchhike and be murdered by a serial killer." He laughs, which seems out of place, but still delights me. His laughter draws me to him.

I take a deep breath and steel up my spine. "Okay, but this is the last time."

"See you in thirty?"

I shake my head. Paul's lack of planning could use changing as well. "Really?"

"Don't worry, I can drive again next week, so you're right, this is the last time."

I wonder if his first trip will be to terrorize Allison, who I hope is his ex. I hope she is older and smarter than me to turn aside Paul's surface charms and see the darkness underneath. A darkness I ignored. A darkness I don't want or need back in my life especially with this guy Bret's awkward intentions. "And you need to stop calling and texting me."

"What about carrier pigeons?" He laughs, a nervous laugh.

"I just can't do *this* again."

"There's no this," he says sharply. "I just thought we were friends now."

I chew on my fingernails as I contemplate a response. What is Paul in my life? He's my past and for sure not my future, but I don't know if he has a place in my present. I never knew him as a friend, just the boy I wanted to kiss. No, the boy that I wanted to kiss me. It was never just about me wanting him, but him wanting me. I needed the affirmation of his attention.

"Like I said, this is the last time," Paul repeats.

"The last time," I echo back, but my memory flashes to the last time I saw Paul at my high school graduation open house. Him giving me another star necklace to replace the one broken during our final fight. Him walking back to his car and me seeing the girl in it with a black eye. That was the last time. I think not of the necklace, but that girl's eye. "Last time."

"I'm out!" I tell mom as I lift the car keys from the table. She looks at her phone.

"It is too early for work," she notices, "Where are you going?

"Like I said, out." I use her my-way-or-highway, no-nonsense tone against her.

She reaches for the Jeep's keys with her left hand. In her right, she holds her cigarette. "You're not taking my car without me knowing where you are going. What are you up to?" She speaks in words meant to wound. The only way to fight back is by giving her the harsh truth.

"I'm giving Paul a ride someplace." I almost beam with pride as she frowns.

"Paul!" She shouts just as I expected. My parents hated Paul, and they didn't even know the whole truth about him raising his hand to me or about us sharing a bed.

I try to downplay it to avoid a fight I regret picking. "He just needs a ride somewhere."

"Doesn't he have friends to do that?" mom asks, flipping her ash into a coffee cup.

I ponder the question since it is one that I have asked myself. To hear Brad tell it, Paul just stopped communicating with him after high school. Brad thought it was because Paul was angry at him for going to California by himself. Paul told me he stayed for me, but I learned that wasn't the truth. It was *another* on his long list of lies.

"I guess not," I finally reply. "So maybe it is good he has someone he can turn to."

"I don't like it, and I don't like him. You were miserable when you were with him."

"You're wrong. I was happy." Part of the time I was happy, but she'll never believe that. I used to think she wanted me to be miserable so she could wear her I-told-you-so face. Now. my seeing him again raises her hackles, and maybe that's the sliver of a reason to help Paul.

"You didn't know better then, but you do now," mom says.

"This is the last time I am seeing him. It is just to give him a ride, that's it. I'm not getting involved with him again." *Involved* isn't the right word. I was never involved with Paul. I was consumed by him in every sense of the word.

She takes a drag on her cigarette. I think about being dragged back into Paul's orbit. Mom and I stare at each other, which we did a lot my senior year. "Your father won't be happy."

I don't disagree with her although my dad seemed less concerned about Paul than he did about Paul's influence on me. An influence which caused my grades to fall and my relationship with my parents to fracture. I broke free of my parents first before I could break free of Paul. "I'm just giving him a ride," I remind her.

"He's using you," she says. "Again."

Obviously, my mom isn't an idiot and knows what teenage boys and girls do. She never inquired, probably because she didn't want to consider the possibility of my having sex with Paul. It didn't jibe with my parents' obedient and innocent version of me they were desperately trying to hang onto, not realizing the more they pushed, the more I pulled away into Paul's arms. I stayed with Paul for too long for all the wrong reasons with spite being one of them.

I sigh deeply, then take the keys. I don't need *this* in my life anymore either. She yells after me, but I walk away and slam the door loudly behind me as my final word on the subject.

Paul looks and sounds dour when I pick him up.

"You okay?" I ask. He climbs in, then pushes himself away from me against the door.

"Fine." He gives me the short answer stiff arm.

"Where are we going?" He gives me an address, not directions. I put it in my GPS and head toward the highway. As I drive through the trailer park where Paul lives, I notice how it looks like nothing has changed other than an increase in 'for sale' signs and overgrown small lawns in front of the doublewides.

"What's wrong?" I ask. It is a question I asked him a lot when we were together.

"I can't believe I have to go to an anger management class!" he shouts.

I wonder at first if he's doing it for ironic comedy, but quickly realize that he's really upset. When he's angry, it is not good for anyone to be around Paul. I push on the gas and merge on the highway, regretting my decision to do this favor for Paul although deep down I knew I wanted to see him again.

I try to change the subject, but he's not having it. Instead, he's in a full-blown rant against the judge, his court appointed attorney, but mostly his ex, Allison. I need to shut this down.

"Look, I don't think you should talk that way about her," I say sharply.

"Why does it bother you? You didn't know that stupid, fat, lying—"

"You shouldn't talk that way about any woman." I recall how Paul talked about and to his mom and sometimes to me. It wasn't pretty. "Maybe this class will help you—"

"You don't learn things in classes," he says, then laughs, his mood a polar opposite. In less than five minutes, he's gone from silent to shouting to cracking jokes. It reminds me that somewhere inside that anger is a good person trapped by negative experiences and bad choices.

As we drive through city streets toward his anger management class, Paul seems anything but angry. He's back joking, desperately trying to get me to laugh, which he succeeds at too easily. "I will become a pirate and put the grr in anger."

I slow down when we near the location, which is a church. Knowing Paul's attitude about religion, this isn't good. He saw his mom become as addicted to TV preachers as his dad was to alcohol, so this location can't make him happy.

"You got a ride home?" I ask, trying to draw yet another line and letting Paul know he can't become dependent on me even though I was once dependent on him for just about everything. I need to end this here and now.

He looks disappointed that I don't offer a ride home, and he's back into angry mode. "I guess I can't count on you for anything, can I?" he snaps.

I flinch but say nothing, letting his harsh words silence me.

"I'm sorry, Star."

These are words he said often to me, but words I've yet to accept. I will never forgive him for hurting me, and I wonder if the word "sorry" is yet another lie. I'm about to explain myself when he decides to hug me. I know better, but I let him embrace me. I don't resist because I also remember how his touch was all that I longed for in my life for so long.

And I know it feels good again to be, if only for a second, back in his arms.

But then I know he must be avoided when I smell the beer on this breath.

After I drop him off, I speed away like someone might from a hit and run, which is how I feel. I was walking along in my life without a care when Paul smashed into me, and now, I'm the injured party.

I wonder if Paul can succeed in anger management, as I wonder if I can control my feelings toward him. Every rational part of my self tells me to run away at full speed, while every emotional part of my soul pulls me toward him. I knew better in high school than to stay with him, but I was trapped, and for a long time, unwilling to chew off my own heart to escape.

As I drive home, I find myself drifting from my bipolar reaction to Paul's intrusion into my life and to Bret, the guy from Flint. I wonder why Bret was at the courthouse, but I'll never get up the nerve to ask. Almost twenty, yet I'm often still tongue tied around boys.

Bret was smart, funny, and odd, exactly the combination that pulls my interest. And he seems to want to know me, which is even better. I wanted to kiss Paul. Now, I want someone who wants to kiss me. I want all the good from Paul, and none of the bad, but I wonder if such a thing is possible. When I get home, I stay in the driveway and look at my copy of *Howl*. I run my finger over Bret's contact info and pick up my phone. Could pushing ten numbers change if not my life, then at least my summer? Could I walk into the light of another rather than get caught back up in the darkness of Paul? I close my eyes, and I try to visualize tomorrow and the day after rather than stay stuck in a past that haunts me still.

I could see myself in Bret's arms, except for one problem. I am still chained to Paul.

4 / Bret

I wonder if there are more views of Radio Free Flint's YouTube videos. I was foolish to think Johanna would bother to look at videos some weird guy told her about in a courtroom hallway no less. The word foolish fits since it describes all my fleeting and frustrating relationships with women since Kylee, not counting sweet yet serious Becca. I fall too deep, too fast, but then get dumped and hurt too easily. Kylee left me a raw nerve.

"Dad, are you about ready?" I yell toward his bedroom. He grunts loudly in response. He was given a day to get things in order before reporting to jail, but the time has come.

I flip through my phone, looking for someone to call, but it is a wasteland. Despite my best efforts, I've failed to bond with anyone at college or at my soul sucking Goodwill job. It seems everyone is too busy or too involved or too something for me. I reach into my past.

"Hey Alex," I say, actually surprised he's answered my call for once.

"Bret, not a good time. I got band practice in just a few minutes."

"Nice of you to squeeze me into your busy schedule," I joke, but he doesn't laugh.

"I'm just busy getting this new band together," he says. I hear music in the background. I listen especially for the bass, wondering who Alex found to take my spot since obviously he's found someone else to fill in as his best friend by the way he usually ignores my calls and texts.

"What's it called? Radio Free Queens?" I joke, but again no laughter in return.

"No, I'm serious about my music now," he says, and the dig hurts.

I don't think he's ever forgiven me for not wanting to take the big risk and leave Flint for New York like he did. I don't even know why I stayed other than it was easier than leaving. "We're called The Qwerty Club."

"So, anything new on the girlfriend front?" I ask. Other than music, the one thing Alex and I could always talk about was girls of every size, shape, and skin color. If Dad had listened to us talk about girls, it would be obvious we weren't gay like he thought. Alex fell hard for Elizabeth, a waitress at The Venus, but it ended when he went to NYC.

"Like I said, I'm busy with the band."

"I get it." I'm a little pissed off by his attitude, but I gotta hang onto Alex. I'm short on other friends except my-ex Becca who seems to be the only person who is close to understanding me. Since Alex is moving into the rear-view, I need to keep Becca front and center.

As always, he doesn't invite me to visit or talk about coming home, so I figure maybe I've seen the last of Alex. All I can hope is that I hear him on the radio or Spotify one day soon. I say my goodbyes and feel positively embarrassed, being made to feel so unwelcome by my so obviously former best friend. It is a good thing Kylee taught me about loss, so I can learn how to handle it as it seems to be my most constant companion.

I hang up from Alex and check the time. Dad's due to report to jail at four, and time is running out. I can't imagine what is going through his mind, and whatever it is, he's not sharing.

"Dad, come on, let's go!" I shout then laugh at myself. Shouting was always dad's job.

I try calling mom, but she's at work. I think she volunteered to work this shift so she wouldn't have to witness this scene, let alone drive dad to jail. Robin is out with friends and it seems she couldn't care less that her father is leaving her life for a hundred days. But then again, when I was sixteen, I hoped that dad would get out of my life. Now that wish has come true, and I hate it. We were at odds, came together for a short time, but then crashed and burned.

I don't hate that he's doing time; that is the consequence of his action, but I hate most that he started drinking again. Eighteen years sober, and then he pissed it all away for no good reason, not that there is ever a good reason to drink. It just makes you stupid, like sex; it warps your perspective, like sex does too. If I'm going to be on my knees, I'd rather be between a woman's legs than hugging a hangover filled toilet.

Dad's clean-shaven and wearing a freshly pressed white shirt with tan slacks. He looks more like he's going to church than to jail. But I guess both demand a need for hope.

"Are you ready to go?" I ask as I reach for my keys.

He stares at me for a second, then his eyes go toward the real estate in front of me. "No, Bret, I'm not." It sounds like he is trying not to cry. He's not the only one.

I meet up with Becca at the Venus Coney Island after I drop dad off and return to Flint. Becca dumped me the summer before we both went to college. She went away to Michigan State while I stayed at home. It is only fifty miles between Flint and East Lansing, but I think she was just looking for an excuse. But since it wasn't a bad breakup, like mine with Kylee, Becca and I stay in touch. Unlike Kylee, Becca was a friend before she became a lover, if only for a brief time. There's no hurt or jealousy, just warm feelings of friendship which I see in her smile that greets me when I walk into the Venus where she waits for me. We hug then head toward a back booth.

We're barely seated before Elizabeth, Alex's ex, brings me coffee like she always does. I signal for a cup for Becca.

"How's work?" Becca asks. It is a nice, safe, neutral subject.

I rattle on about nothing important, listing all the usual complaints anyone has about work: bad hours, crappy pay, annoying coworkers, worse boss. She tries to act interested.

"Are you doing a play this summer?" she asks for a slightly more interesting topic.

"I tried out and didn't make it," I confess.

Elizabeth brings Becca coffee. I try to ignore the heavy amounts of cream and sugar Becca puts in the fine dark brown brew. I rattle on more about not getting a part in the play.

"Wow, that's amazing," Becca says. "You starred in every play in high school."

I don't need the reminder that I used to be a big deal, and now I'm lucky if I make the cut, and even then, I don't get a decent part. "As my theater teacher, Mr. Douglas, used to say, 'There are no small parts, just ones with fewer lines.' That's me now, except I don't have any lines."

Becca smiles politely. She starts talking about her summer Halo Burger job. I try to pay attention, but I keep flashing back to high school. Back to this place where I shared so many good times with Alex and Sean until Sean betrayed me by sleeping with Kylee. Always Kylee.

"Can I ask you something, but you totally don't need to answer?" I ask.

She gives me a skeptical look. "I guess." She looks pretty with her curly brown hair despite her ugly red and yellow Halo Burger uniform. With her smarts and sweetness, it was easy to see why I was attracted to her. I wish we would have lasted longer, but the timing was wrong on so many levels. Some people are just not meant to be together.

"I know we broke-up because you went away to school, but was it more than that?"

She sips her coffee again and stares at the table, refusing to make eye contact.

"Look, you can say whatever. I won't be hurt." I know there is no hurt I could ever experience as big as when Kylee cheated on me.

"Honestly Bret?"

"One hundred percent."

I brace myself for the blow, but she smiles. "You were like horny all the time, so that was a challenge." My face flushes in embarrassment even though she's telling the truth. I still am that way, and maybe that's not such a good thing. Kylee got me hooked on hooking up.

"I was a normal seventeen-year-old," is my weak defense.

"But really, you were on me about it from day one."

"That was the idea: to be on you or under you. You know I didn't have a preference."

She laughs and joins me in the blush brigade.

"I mean didn't other guys go—" I start, but she shushes me.

"This is about you. You wanted to know, so I'm telling you. If it helps, then good."

I flash on Kylee though I never understood why she needed to break my heart. I flash on Johanna from the court hallway and wonder if I should give another woman a chance to break my heart again.

"And you were so jealous whenever I talked with another guy. I mean, I knew that was why we couldn't do the long-distance thing. Even during our senior year, any time I'd talk to another guy, you would—"

"Get all jealous and angry, I know." Yet another Kylee scar never totally healed.

"That's it. There's nothing wrong with you, Bret. You were just young. Heck, so was I."

I wish I had gained some wisdom since Kylee, but my emotional soul is scorched earth.

"Thanks, Becca. And you were the best, just in case you were wondering. I mean—"

"But I wasn't Kylee, was I?" she asks, and we both know there's no answer to this question that ends well for either of us, so it just sits there wallowing like a walrus in the mud.

After she drops the Kylee bomb, things get real awkward real quick, and we both sense it. We talk some more, make some half-assed plans to meet again, then finish our coffee. She gets up to leave, so I hug her goodbye, but there's no electricity between us. We're drained.

I sit in the Metro in The Venus parking lot. I am in a time machine back to over two years ago. Dad was working and not drinking. I was in love and not hurting. I was something strong.

I pull out my phone and go to my favorite Radio Free Flint video, which I watch for the hundredth time it seems.

Me, Alex, and Sean playing and Kylee dancing. Then and forever, but not now. Not now.

5 / *Johanna*

"So, Jo, you haven't messaged him?" Sydney asks. We're having coffee at the Starbucks in the Villages of Rochester Hills before she goes to work. Unlike most malls around Detroit, this one has lots of people shopping – well, white people shopping since it is the Detroit suburbs.

"No." Ever since I told Sydney about Bret, she seems more excited than I am. I am mostly scared of rejection, something I thought I overcame when I asked Paul to kiss me.

"I mean, what are you waiting for?" She taps her bright white coffee cup with her short, chewed nails. Her dyed-red hair is buried under a redder bandana while she wears her National Coney Island green uniform. At least the color of it matches her tired looking eyes.

"Maybe to be confident like you," I answer. It was actually being confident enough to ask Paul to kiss me that led to everything as I appeared desperate, and he used it against me.

"Girl, you got it all. You got brains and beauty. You just need a little bravado!"

"Brains, maybe. The other two, not so much."

On the way over to Starbucks, I passed by the Gap where my old pal Kara was working. We waved at each other, but that was it. Kara, Brad's ex, always intimidated me even after we became friends for a short period of time before the difference between us became too much to bridge. I recall how another old friend, Pam, once said, "Kara is great looks, and you are great books" that led to a permanent inferiority complex about my appearance and my confidence, both of which Kara had in spades. I tried to reconnect with Kara when I got home, but she'd moved on with her life like I wish I had with mine.

"What are you waiting for?" Sydney presses, sounding super excited for me. "I mean, it sounds like he was into you. I mean, talking about beat poetry at a first meeting. How hot is that?"

"What are you waiting for?" I counter. "Do you have a boyfriend this summer?"

"No." She seems sad when she says it. Maybe that's why she's so behind this idea. Sydney told me she is sitting the summer out boyfriend-wise and focusing on working as much as she can to earn money to go back to Columbia. Unlike me, she doesn't have a scholarship, so whatever she makes at the National Coney Island goes right into the college fund.

"Look I don't know what that was, but guys don't hit on me." Paul didn't hit on me; in fact, it is quite the opposite. He was the outgoing senior cut-up; I was the shy, serious student, one year younger. Opposites didn't just attract, we locked together like immovable magnets. I guess what surprised me most about this Bret guy was that I was worth his time, attention, and attraction. If he was here, I would tell him the feeling was mutual and even more.

"But Jo, he *did* hit on you. Why can't you—"

I cut her off before she goes there. "Roman, Marcus, none of them. I'm not like Kara. I'm not like you. I'm just not going to be that girl that guys hit on. I accept that."

She laughs. "Then why can't you accept this guy Bret did hit on you?"

"I don't want to appear desperate again," I mumble.

Sydney reaches for my phone. "It's not desperate, it's desire, baby. If you don't message him, then I will!" I hold on tight to my phone because Sydney is liable to do anything.

"I don't *need* a boyfriend," I protest a little too much.

"Yea, Jo, but you *want* one," Sydney counters.

She's right, but I'm not going to let her know as that's my secret shame. I never really had a serious boyfriend until Paul, and then, he devastated me. I rebounded quickly with Marcus and then hooked up way too quickly with Roman at college. It is too hard not to want one, and despite my still amazing lack of self-confidence, I know that it has not been that hard to find one even if I take the first step. Like I did with Paul, like I'll have to do now with Bret.

Sydney points at my phone. "So do you contact him or do I?"

"I will." I text Bret a simple greeting, then I play the waiting game of watching three dots bounce like small punches to the stomach as I wait for him to respond.

Bret responds quickly to my message. I start a return text, delete it, then start another, but everything sounds wrong. Only a person's voice sounds right so I dial his number

"Bret, it's Johanna from Pontiac," I start, and already I screwed up like he knew another Johanna from some other city. For someone so smart, I can be so dumb, as mom reminds me.

"I was hoping you would contact me," Bret says. I hope he is smiling.

"I just really hate to text." You can't hear someone laugh over text. Of all the things I miss about Paul, his ability to make me laugh seems like the biggest hole in my life.

"Me, too," Bret says. "Could you imagine if Shakespeare texted or tweeted? We'd have memes and tweets instead of plays and sonnets. 'To be or not to be' would be a cat gif."

"But I see you tweet a lot." I didn't tell Sydney how I had been silently stalking Bret on his social media. "You certainly have a lot to say about music, most of it not good."

I recall Paul, ranting about any music that wasn't Springsteen, and soon he had me doing the same. I let Paul become the Boss of me even in my musical tastes.

"Well, I was in a band," he says proudly. "Did you watch any of my videos?"

"I will as soon as we hang up." I admit and feel embarrassed for not doing it sooner.

"But I can't wait three hours until we're done talking. I want it now."

"I don't know much about music," I say, withholding my near encyclopedic knowledge of Springsteen thanks to Paul's obsession. "But I'll check it out."

"I don't have a band anymore. That was more of a high school thing. Now, I'm all serious about being a working man at Goodwill. Are you working this summer?"

"At the Barnes & Noble at the Villages in Rochester Hills."

"Maybe I'll need to check that out. There's a B & N at Flint's Genesee Valley Mall, but I'd rather haunt Jellybean Used Books and Records for lost treasures and underground finds."

"Well, what we say at work is if you want to check a book out, then go to the library."

"I'd rather see you, Johanna, instead of the library." My heart skips from his flirting.

I pause for a second and put my hand over the phone. "He wants to see me." Sydney gives me an over exaggerated thumbs up, then starts making kissing noises. She's impossible.

"So, what do you think? Can I get a vision of you up close and personal?"

"How up close? How personal?" I fire right back at him.

"I guess that's for you to decide," he says softly, almost a whisper.

There's something in his seductive tone that sounds familiar, too familiar. I shiver. Maybe this isn't such a good idea after all, but then again, spending the summer alone doesn't seem like such a good idea either. "So maybe I'll come down to visit sometime," he says.

"When?" I regret my eager tone as soon as the word leaves my mouth.

"Pontiac is like fifty miles, so that means fifteen minutes in Michigan drive-time."

I laugh, which causes Sydney to do the same. "Well, I get off work at six."

"I don't know Pontiac. Why leave all the beauty that is Flint? You think of someplace to meet and go. You can lead me like a horse to water, and I bet you can make me drink."

I flash on the smell of Paul getting out of my car. Paul's drinking wasn't the cause of his problems—I don't think I ever understood what the cause of his problems except maybe the trauma of his dad was leaving him—but it sure didn't help. Beer let loose the monster inside of him.

"Call me when you get down here, and I'll think of someplace," I say.

"Well, I guess you could say it's a date. How adult of us."

"Does that mean we are committing adultery?" I ask.

He groans, but in a good way. Paul's non-stop pun fests normally generated the same response. Then it hits me: is this guy Bret like Paul, and if he is, is that a good thing or a bad thing? Can there be someone who is only the good side of Paul, or do you need both sides of the coin to make the man?

"I'll see you soon, Johanna," Bret says. I like to hear a cute boy say my name.

As soon as I hang up the phone, Sydney wants all the details, but I tell her to wait. I search Radio Free Flint on YouTube, and watch several videos, most of which seem to be from the same location. It looks like they were shot in front of a Kmart department store. I stare intently as the longest video, and even though it is grainy and dark, I can tell that Bret has natural stage charisma. Most of the videos are of just the band, but this long one focuses more on the crowd than the stage. When the camera is on the stage, I see how Bret, even while singing, has his eyes all over this pretty girl dancing like some punk ballerina. There's two other people on the stage with Bret and another fifty in the audience, but from the way Bret is looking at the dazzling dancer, it is like they are the only two people in the world.

6 / Bret

It's a ritual that I can't escape, even as I get ready to drive to Pontiac to meet Johanna for the first time. I need to see it like some sort of touchstone that pulls me into the past, so I can fortify myself for the present. It is like I am cursed by the gods. I cannot bear to see what I must see. Just before getting on the expressway, I detour down 12th street, then turn down the alley by the railroad tracks. There at the dead end of the alley is a railroad overpass wall filled with graffiti. It overflows with gang signs, but underneath I still see it: "Bret Lives." Once it said, "Bret Lives Kylee," because the word love was too common for someone as special as Kylee. But after she cheated on me with Sean, I changed the writing on the wall by hammering away her name and affirming that, after her betrayal, I still mattered. Like the video of her dancing, I view this message almost every day. You can't go anyplace new, I suppose, until you know where you've been. I've taken many a hard-luck detour on this human highway. I need that reminder today more than ever as I think about dad's hard-luck life and how luck seemed to have finally turned bad for him but good for me. "Bret Lives" is mostly covered over, but I believe it. I wonder if, because of this Johanna girl, that it might one day read "Bret Lives Again."

"So where to, Johanna?" I ask when Johanna climbs in my old beat-up Chevy, which is about all everybody in Flint drives these days. I pick her up at her work, and she looks the part, all dressed up for success in a powder-blue, button-down blouse and khakis, while I'm in my normal goofy Goodwill t-shirt and worn jeans. "I got gas in the car and no place else to go."

"How about a coffee shop?" she asks. I shake my head in an exaggerated fashion.

"Played and cliched." I say, trying to sound witty, which I just sense this girl appreciates.

She suggests a few other cafes and restaurants, but I don't want the distraction of other people. She mentions some bars around that let in people under 21 but mainly for dancing. Any kind of dancing reminds me of Kylee and how no one can compare to her. Besides, all I know how to do is slow dance, which I can barely manage, and while I'm interested in body-to-body contact, I don't know if she is. I think about what Becca said about me and sex. I don't disagree, but I don't know if it is something I can change. Sex is like a drug that, once you've experienced the rush, it is hard to forget it and not want it again as soon and as often as possible.

"I don't really know any other place to suggest," she says, then sighs.

I point up. "It's a nice night. Have you got any lakes around here?" I ask, all casual like I didn't already have an image of us lying on a beach staring at the stars.

"I think there's a park at one in Waterford a few miles away. You plan on going fishing?"

"Depends what's on the other end of the hook." She blushes at my overt flirting. "Is there a beach there?"

"I guess, but I don't know. I'd rather dive into a book than the water," Johanna says.

"Like *Howl*. Did you ever finish it?'

"I thought you might ask," she says.

I look over at her. She recites the last line of the poem word-for-word.

"Not bad, not bad." I touch her leg, and my hands tingle with human touch, but she pulls away. "You know I write poetry, too, and wrote most of the lyrics for my band." The last part is a lie as most of the songs of Radio Free Flint were Alex's although I offered up a line or two. She'll never know, and it feels good to boast about something even if it is in my past.

"I write for the Columbia school paper," she says, sounding quite proud of herself.

"You go to Columbia?" I think how rinky-dink U of M Flint hardly compares.

"I'm studying journalism," she says. "I was editor of my high school paper."

I laugh way too loud. "I got a grudge against school newspapers. I almost got expelled from school because of something I wrote for mine." I tell her the story about a controversial editorial I wrote about bullying at my school and how school tried to kick me out. I managed to stay in school thanks to the ACLU and Kylee's mom who made my principal back down. I don't mention the part about Kylee's mom. I plan not to mention Kylee's name all night.

"That's a great story," Johanna says.

"I got lots of them, mainly about me getting in trouble for being a resident oddball."

"I never really fit in either," she says.

"Smart as you are, it was probably because you got A's in every class."

"Not in every class and not every year." She still sounds depressed about it.

"We're both square pegs," I say. "Maybe that means we can fit each other."

"There's the sign for the park," she says as we exit the highway.

"Look, it is a nice clear night, so you can see the stars. You can't see them in Flint. There's like an industrial fog all over the city. It goes nice with the poisoned drinking water. Yes, my hometown has it all."

"Pontiac is no picnic, promise," she adds. I smile at the amazing alliteration.

We start to compare our hometowns, almost trying to top—or bottom—one another, but the competition is friendly. Everything about this girl, except for how she pulled her leg away, is friendly. I made the right choice, making the trip, but still need to see if it is worth it.

"Let's park there." I point to a spot in a lot by the lake beach. Since it is early evening, there are just a few other cars around. I park, and we get out of the car. She looks hesitant, even more so when I pull out a beach blanket I'd stashed in the trunk for just such an occasion. I drape the blanket over my shoulders and start imagining us horizontal rather than vertical.

"How about we do a walk and talk?" I ask. We walk a bit, then I take off my green Chucks and socks when we get to the beach. She does the same. Naked feet are at least a start.

We walk around the beach barefoot. I put my hand out like bait, but she doesn't take it.

"So, Columbia, what is that like?" I ask and she's quickly into telling me stories about her time in New York. I'd like to hear such stories about life in New York from Alex, but that relationship teeters on collapse. Besides, if it isn't all about Alex's band, then it is not worth talking about. I perk up when she mentions hanging out with someone named Sydney.

"Boy, girl, or city in Australia?" And I wonder if Johanna has a boyfriend or a girlfriend. I wonder if I've misjudged the situation, something I have quite the experience doing.

"Girlfriend, and no, not like that."

"So, you're not dating anyone?" I ask as waves lap on our feet. I hold my breath.

"You?" is her counteroffer. I shrug my shoulders and put my hand closer. This time she takes it, wrapping her fingers with mine. Human connection sparks me like a lighter.

We walk a little more, then take in the sunset. It's peaceful and a far cry from noise in my life. Maybe that—and her hand in mine—is what makes everything seem cool and calm.

As the night starts to fall from the sky, I ask her to sit on the beach blanket with me, but she says she needs to get going. I wonder does she have someplace to go or if she is just done with me?

We walk back to the car, our hands no longer touching. As she waits for me to open the door, I move closer and try to kiss her. She turns away. "Something wrong, Johanna?"

"I don't know you."

"Do you know a better way to get to know someone?" I arch an eyebrow.

"I just—"

"It's fun, and it's free. Tell me; can you find a better bargain even at Goodwill?"

She laughs. Good. Smiles. Better. I move closer to kiss her, and she complies. Best. It doesn't last long but just enough to remind me of what I've been missing and how hungry I am.

My heart growls from emptiness.

We kiss more; then, she says she needs to get home. I don't argue. Even if I didn't do well in school at science, I know and can feel chemistry.

"I had a nice time," she says as we head out.

"I had a great time, too." I ache at how these words fall short of long-lost feelings.

"You should come visit again," she says with a smile. A bright, wide, inviting smile.

"I'll take you up on that offer. How is tomorrow morning?" I try to strike a tone between desperation and desire. I don't tell her I need to be in Pontiac for less desirable reasons anyway.

I drive under the speed limit, so it takes as long as possible to get her back to her car. Along the way, I share more stories about high school hijinks while she mostly focuses on her frosh year at Columbia. We rode two very different wheels, but I sense our spokes clicked.

When we get to her car, there's a brief but longer kiss before she leaves my Chevy. It is the kind of kiss that lasts a lot longer than it takes. The best kind.

I wait to make sure she gets in her car okay before I head home. I honk once like an idiot, plug in my phone, and kick out a playlist of classic English punk. I scream along in delight.

It is a long drive home, so I think about lighting up, but then I realize I still have the taste of Johanna on my lips, and I feel like I'm already high.

7 / *Johanna*

"I liked what you said," I say to Bret from across the small table at Starbucks. There's a coffee shop part of Barnes & Noble, but I don't want to go there before my work shift starts. Bret only waited twelve hours before visiting again, which was about eleven hours too long. I think he agreed to a coffee shop because it was convenient for me. Give him another point.

"I find that hard to believe since I say mostly stupid stuff." Bret then makes a goofy face.

"That part about us being square pegs." I sip my sugary coffee. Since Bret was buying, I didn't want to order my normal expensive and fattening desert-disguised-as-coffee drink.

"I spent four years in high school getting beat down by my angry father and asshole high school bullies. I got hammered, but not drunk."

I hope he's not lying. Having lived through one relationship with an alcoholic, I don't have the courage or patience to do it again. "Because of how you dressed?"

"This mess?" He points at his 'McLovin' t-shirt and oversized camouflage Army pants.

"I'm sure that didn't help," I say, but not in a nasty way.

"People beat me down not for what I wore but for who I was."

I lean across the table. "And who was Bret Hendricks?"

"Well, like you said when we met, I'm a scholar, singer, and wrestling fan. Also, I was a star of the stage. We did six plays a year, and I normally had the lead in all of them."

"Six plays? Isn't that a lot?" I remember we only did three at Pontiac West.

"Well, what we lacked in quality we made up for in quantity," he cracks.

I almost spit coffee from my mouth, and it's good I don't do that. Not only because it is embarrassing, but Paul used to take it as a singular mission to get me to laugh so hard that I would expel a beverage. I don't need any memories of Paul sharing this table with Bret.

"I mostly just wrote for the newspaper," I tell him, playing it modest. I not only was editor of my paper, but I also won a couple of state journalism awards, which helped me land the scholarship at Columbia. Bragging is not an attractive trait, and more than anything, I want to appear attractive to Bret even if I'm in my boring, white button-down and khakis work outfit.

"You work in a bookstore, so do you read a lot too?" Bret asks.

I pause, thinking about how to play this. I do read a lot, but for some guys, this casts me as the quirky nerd girl, and they will never look at me in any other light. Finally, I say, "Some. How about your reading?" The safest way to avoid an answer is with a question.

Bret turns over his phone, looks something up, then shows me a list of authors he's read, from classic greats like Steinbeck to out-there authors like Pynchon, Vonnegut, and Palahniuk. There are also authors like Camus, Kafka, and Sartre. The words gush out of him like he's just been waiting for someone to ask him that question. "How about you? Who do you read?"

I don't respond by listing my favorites, which all seem to involve strong women warriors destroying dragons and demons in eight hundred plus pages. "That is quite the list."

"I used to own lots of books. Then—" Bret starts to say, then cuts himself off.

"What happened to them?"

Bret sips his black coffee slowly as a way to avoid answering. I let it go.

I glance at my phone. "I only have ten minutes before I need to start work."

Bret sets his coffee down and reaches his hand across the table. I touch just his fingertips, and it's enough for me to know there's a something between us I can't describe, but certainly feel.

"Well, could we put those ten minutes to better use?" he asks, then winks.

I shake my head and then do an exaggerated sigh. "Is that all you think about?" I'm half-joking and half-serious. I like Bret and want to show that, but I know from Paul how getting physically involved too quickly with someone wraps your heart up in chains and locks.

"Want to go out to my car?" he asks. "I'm parked close."

"I'm good," I say, trying to cool this hot coffee down, at least for this moment.

"Well, can I at least walk you to work?" Bret says, sounding if not angry then miffed.

"Bret, I do want to kiss you again," I admit and feel better for doing so when he smiles.

I take the last big gulp from coffee, and he does the same. We return the cups to the counter. He puts out his hand, and I gently take hold of it. We walk slowly back to the store. Along the way, Bret makes fun of the mall walkers for being too old, too rich, and too white.

When we get to the store, Bret looks at his phone, then shows it to me. It is one to ten.

"So, I guess I just have one minute left before work starts." I say then sigh.

"One long minute," he whispers.

I lean into him. "Any ideas of what we should do with that one minute?"

"I can't think of anything." Bret says just before he kisses me. I know two things by the time we are done kissing: I am late for work, and I can't wait to see Bret again

8 / Bret

It takes forever, it seems, to work my way through the visiting process at Oakland County Jail. It is almost like they want you to be angry at your loved ones with all the rules and hassles you have to endure to get to the visiting area, including a long line at the screening station.

Once inside, I realize the visit will be nothing more than a fuzzy Facetime call since I can only communicate with dad through a phone while looking through a dirty pane of glass.

Dad's already sitting there when I arrive. I sense from his furrowed brow that he, the least patient man in America, has been waiting for me. Sometimes I think Dad takes all the anger at his life gone wrong, wraps it in a ball and throws it at me. I am close, and I don't fight back, so I am an easy target.

"Glad you could make it," is his opening, open-handed slap to my face.

I try explaining the process, but he doesn't seem interested. "Where's your mother?"

"Working." Which is almost always the answer when someone asks where mom is.

"And your sister?"

I shrug my shoulders. He shakes his head. We are the frustration mimes.

"How's the food?" I ask having no idea what you ask someone in jail. Sitting on the other side of this barrier is no place I ever thought I'd be. "Not as good as The Venus I bet."

I hope this would elicit if not a laugh, then at least a smile, but there's none. Like he did a lot during my high school years, dad just looks through me like I'm some sort of space alien.

"You doing AA in here?" I ask, desperate for something to talk about with him.

"Did you think I wouldn't?" he snaps back in full defensive mode. It must be the fear.

"No, I just wondered if—"

"You should mind your own business, Bret."

"I just thought that—"

"You don't think, Bret; that's your whole problem. You just waltz through life with your stupid music and your silly clothes not thinking about the things that a man thinks about."

"You don't know half of it." Dad doesn't know about most of my life not because I'm unwilling to share but because he's not interested. The phone jiggles in my shaking hand.

"I think I know a lot more about a man's life than you do. Trust me, mister," dad says.

I want to ask why he's so angry at me, but I just sense that will lead to more verbal abuse, so I change the subject. "So, I met this girl from Pontiac—"

"So, you came to see me on your way to getting laid?"

"Dad, no. It's not like that." Although the idea of getting laid is always on my mind.

"Can't you get anything right?" Dad should have a fire-breathing snout installed.

"I don't know what you want from me?" I am almost in tears from frustration.

"Man up. Start with that, Bret. For once in your life, man up."

I thought these were the cruelest words he could say, but he tops them easily by saying, "Guard, I'm done here."

9 / Johanna

I've just finished my shift, and I'm making arrangements to meet with Sydney to tell her all about my visits with Bret when I see standing by the front door at work – Paul.

"Hey, Joha, how was work?" He asks casually, like we're friends or something. What we are I guess I still haven't figured out. How can someone relegated to your past still be part of your life? What does he want? More importantly, do I want anything from him other than to leave me alone? It is a moth-to-a-flame situation, and I know my wings are too thin and fragile.

"Paul, what are you doing here?" I ask, not so casually, but with a strict tone.

He looks hurt. It's a trump card he used to play often and always with great effect. "I just thought I'd see how you were doing, and I wanted to share some news, that's all. No big deal."

"It is a big deal, Paul," I say, finding some inner strength. "You just can't show up at my work. I helped you out, but that's it between us. Last time was the last time."

"I know that, Star. I just wanted to show you something. Follow me, please?" He asks rather than commands. I should turn him away, yet I follow him out of bad habit.

"I don't have time. I have someplace to be." That place is the other end of the phone with Bret. We've talked every day since we kissed again plus exchanged texts and photos.

"Look, it will take just a minute; that's all I need from you. You don't have one minute in your life for me?" Paul always knew how to get me to ride the guilt train.

We head out to the parking lot, me two steps behind until we get to it. The black Firebird. The car I couldn't stop looking for on the streets of Pontiac. It wasn't until I moved to New York that I gave up the habit of Firebird watching.

"I got my license back, so the Bird is ready to fly!"

I don't ask why he lost his license A DUI I assume. Maybe it is best I don't know.

He beams with joy. "You want to take a ride Star?"

"I can't." And I won't. I need to brace myself for his attempts at connection like I used to brace myself for his bitter tongue and bruising rough hands. "I need to go."

He answers by opening the door, inviting me inside like he was deaf to me. But I'm not blind when I see him pull out a pint of ice cream and a dozen roses. Like old times. Like good times. Like bad times. Like Paul times.

"I wanted to thank you for helping me out." He reaches out to hand me the gifts, but I keep my hands at my side. I will not be taken in by taking these things from him.

"Look, Star, I'm just trying to be nice, that's all." He looks hurt, wounded, lost.

"I know that, but I just can't accept these things. It would be sending you the wrong message. We're over, and we are never getting back together; you know that right?"

"Like I said, I was just thanking you," he grumbles. "If you don't want them, fine." He hurls the roses on the pavement, followed by the ice cream. He quickly stomps on the ice cream, expelling it from the carton all over the pavement.

I don't ask him if he's still in anger management class because if he is, it isn't taking. "And this is why. You haven't changed and that scares me. It should scare you, too."

He glares at me with all too familiar blue eyes of red-hot hate, then kicks the empty carton before grinding up the roses under his feet. "Fuck you, Johanna, fuck you!"

He races to the other side of the car, unlocks the door, and turns on the Bird. Just like he used to leave my driveway, he revs the engine, turns up the Springsteen, and then steps on the gas hard. I watch him speed through the parking lot out toward the street on his way to nowhere.

"So that's it," I tell Sydney about Paul. She's just finished her shift at National Coney Island, and we're sharing a table there. She wipes the sweat from her brow with a paper napkin.

"You can't let him do any of this to you."

"I didn't, I told you how—"

"You should have never even spoken with him. He needs to be a ghost."

I sip my coffee, cream, and sugar mix. "I know that now."

"Did you really think he had changed?" she asks in full prosecutor mode.

"Maybe."

"Some people change, some don't. It's great you are not the person you were in high school because, from what you've told me, you might just have gotten in that car with him."

"You don't understand," I say, unsure if I understand anything at all. "It was so intense between us. I remember all the bad stuff, but the good times keep coming into focus."

"Then you need new glasses," she scolds me like my mother would. I would hate her for it if she wasn't probably right. 'Probably' isn't the word I need, but certainty. I thought I had closure with Paul, but the fact I'm still talking about him proves I do not.

"If he approaches you again, then you have to do something." Sydney says all serious.

"I told him to leave me alone, and I meant it this time. He's gone."

Sydney reaches across the table and taps her finger on my chest, just below the star necklace. "Sure he is, Jo, you just keep on believing that, but I'm not buying it. When you don't mention his name, then we'll have something, but until then, consider yourself hooked."

I shake my head. The day's too much to take in when my phone buzzes.

"It's Bret," I tell Sydney. She does a school-girl giggle, which cracks me up. I'm laughing when I answer the phone. "Hey, what's up?" I pull myself together to be all cool and collected, although as I've yet to tell Sydney and even admit to myself, our kisses were hot.

"You busy now?"

I look over at Sydney but think about Paul. "No, come on down." I know the only way to rid myself of the dark shadow of the past is to walk into the bright light of the present.

I leave Sydney with plenty of confident advice about dating from a girl currently without a boyfriend. I drive home in the Jeep but decide to detour through the memories of my life.

I drive by the post office where in a mad fit of rage I mailed Paul all of the ashes of the gifts he gave me. I drive by the public library where Paul would pick me up after studying chemistry only to study anatomy in the backseat of his car. I can't leave out my high school, so I drive by Pontiac West where so many good things happened and just as many bad. The same can be said of Santi's Pizza where Paul first lashed out at me only to bring me gifts to make up for his bad behavior. I do a quick drive by my grandparent's house where we hooked up for the first time or made love as I thought of it then in my sentimental high school haze. I park briefly outside of the trailer park where Paul lives with his mom just like I did two years ago and the place where he hooked up with me often, if always unsatisfyingly. I drive over to the mini-storage place where Paul drank and where we broke-up to the sounds of Springsteen's "Backstreets" blaring in the background. I head down the road from my house to one of the places we used to go parking. Gazing over the stretch of deserted road, I think of Paul and me locked in a passionate embrace. I finally end the tour in my driveway where my greatest mistake was letting Paul back into my life. I walk into the quiet house, but as soon as I get to my bedroom, I fill it with tears. Tears I still taste full of anger and bitterness that I can't let go off because of Paul

I am happy to welcome Bret into my life in the present. I just can't let him know it is already occupied with a chain-rattling ghost from my past.

10 / Bret

"I'm going to see her now," I tell Alex. He says nothing, showing his disinterest in anything that isn't about him or his music. I wonder why I call and why he even picks up. Am I a pity friend? Is he answering out of guilt or obligation rather than friendship?

I hear music in the background. Alex talks over it. "What is she like?" he asks blandly.

I start to describe Johanna but realize halfway through that I don't know that much about her other than I am deeply attracted to her and full of major lustful thoughts about her.

"You guys fuck yet?" Alex asks.

"We've only seen each other once," I remind Alex.

"So, she's not like Kylee?" he asks. It is nice to know that Alex's view of Kylee remains unchanged after two years. He didn't just not like her, he loathed her. He found her clove cigarette smoking, journal keeping persona to be pretentious, but mostly he found her a distraction to my time playing in his band. It was never our band; it was always his band. When Sean suggested Kylee sing in the band, I thought Alex was going to stroke out.

"What, too soon?" Alex jokes, but I don't respond with a laugh. As I once told him, how to move girls from the vertical to the horizontal was one of life's great mysteries until Kylee. Unlike my one previous girlfriend, Kylee wasn't shy about her body or sharing it. We hadn't been together even a month before we hooked-up the first time. After that, it was a regular occurrence, sometimes at her parents' house even when they were home. Those were the days.

"Johanna's like you, Alex, a sophisticated New Yorker, so I'm sure it won't last long."

"I assumed she was from Michigan."

"She is, but she goes to Columbia."

This sets Alex off on a rant against Ivy League schools. Alex probably could have gotten into one, but instead, he mortgaged his college future, moving to New York for his music.

"When she's back in school in New York this fall, I'll tell her to check out my new band The Qwerty Club."

Then it hits me. I am staying here, and she is going back this fall to college in New York.

I will barely have a chance to know this girl before she moves away.

"I gotta go and get this mess together," Alex says sounding bored with me.

"I could say the same about my life," I crack. He laughs, then hangs up, leaving me alone on I-75 with my thoughts, which I try to move from images of Kylee to visions of Johanna.

I honk the horn, and Johanna emerges from her parent's house. She wears a light blue Columbia t-shirt, dark blue jeans, her B & W Chucks, and a Detroit Tigers baseball cap. She's sporting sunglasses and a big smile when she climbs inside. I kiss her on the cheek when she sits down. She doesn't resist, but she doesn't move in for more. Not a good sign.

"So, you don't want me to meet your parents?" I ask as I back out of the driveway of a typical big suburban house. A far cry from the small house that I call home. A home the bank owns and could kick us to the curb at any moment if mom loses one of her jobs.

"That's not a good idea, meeting my parents," she says.

I flip my tinted green ponytail her way. "Too much?"

"I'm nineteen and in college. They don't get to say whom I date."

"So, this is another date?"

Johanna laughs. It's a Goldilocks' laugh – not too hard, not too soft, just right. "Well, I thought it was. If not, then what would you call it?"

"I guess that depends." I reach out and touch her leg. She doesn't knock my hand away. I keep it there as we drive back to the park. We talk about nothing important again, but the conversation moves quickly, never stalls. She keeps up, or maybe it is the other way around.

As I touch her leg, it just makes me want to touch her even more with much fewer clothes. Johanna's so different from Kylee, except in one way I hope, meaning that a hook-up is in the near future, not some act relegated to my past.

I wait until we get to the park. We get out of the car and walk hand in hand down to the beach. There are a few families finishing up the day, but other than that, the landscape is ours. I carry that beach blanket with me and toss it down on the sand. I sit and invite her to join me. She does that raised eyebrow thing again, sighs, but then sits down next to me. I pull her next to me, but she's not buying everything that I'm selling.

"So. your parents wouldn't be a big fan of me?" I ask.

"Honest, I didn't tell them about you. It's not their business. You?"

"I don't have a normal home life," I say, then play the sympathy card. "My dad's actually in jail right now." I can sense her body tense. "That's why I was at the courthouse that day."

"Bret, I'm sorry." She rubs my left shoulder. It feels nice.

"He's in for a hundred days for causing an accident when he was driving drunk. He's an alcoholic and—"

"Does the apple fall far from the tree?"

"Not me. I smoke a little, but that's it. I don't like that feeling of losing control," I say. "Most of the people in theater get high, so I join them, but it's not my thing."

"What is your thing?" she asks. I take off her hat and set it aside.

I shift my body so that I'm face to face, then lip to lip with her. "This."

We kiss for a while, and then I gently pull her back on the blanket with me. While it's been a while, my lips and tongue both seem to remember what to do. "You like?"

She just takes her glasses off and kisses me, hard. I rub my hands through her hair, down the side of her face, then the length of her body. My lips and tongue work her mouth while my hands caress her body. I pull her on top of me, then press her body against mine. It feels good to feel the weight of another person. My heart beats faster and blood rushes south.

She must feel it because she moves off me, quickly. "Let's slow down."

"That would be easy to do if we had a lot of time, but you're going back to school after the summer, right?" She nods. "So slow doesn't really work for me. Does it work for you?"

She puts her glasses back on, then her ball cap. "I think we should go."

"Johanna, look, it's no big thing. I mean what else is there to do in Pontiac?"

"I think maybe you've got the wrong idea." She stands up. I follow her lead.

"No, I have the right idea," I counter. "Look, I got a shitty job and a dad in jail. I didn't get a part in the summer production, and my best friend is mostly ghosting me. So, it seems like I've got shit all around me, but you're a bright light. You're smart, pretty, funny and—"

"Look, you say those things, but you don't know me. That's who you want me to be."

"I guess I feel better about you than you do yourself," I snap back.

"Don't go there."

"Look, I'm being a jerk. I'm sorry. I thought this would be fun, that's it."

She shakes her head, then turns her back on me and walks to the car. I pick up the blanket then follow her with cement feet. I let her inside the car but don't say a word. I drive to her house in the silence of resentment and regret, two intense emotions I know all too well.

When I pull down her street, I finally speak. "Look, I'm sorry. I didn't think."

She taps the side of my head with her right index finger. "You're right."

"So let me ask you something. How come you were at that courthouse?" I ask.

She taps me again. "Again, with the not thinking. That's not your concern."

"I opened up to you."

"I think you opened up just to get my legs open." She laughs when she says it.

"Maybe a little. Is that so wrong?" I am so busted.

"No, Bret, it's just too soon," she says as I get ready to pull into her driveway.

"*Mea culpa.* Which is Latin for 'I fucked up bad,'" I say. "Even so, will you see me again?"

"Keep driving!" she shouts as a non-answer.

"What's wrong?"

"Just keep driving, okay, please," she pleads. "Around the block, anything!"

I stop, turn, and head back down the street. She's nearly hysterical. I don't ask why. Instead, I just look in the rearview at what could be so scary. It's a normal suburban home with three cars parked out in the driveway: two big white Jeeps and one beaten-up black Firebird.

11 / *Johanna*

We circle the neighborhood several times before I see Paul's Firebird has flown from my house and I tell Bret it is okay to take me home.

"Is everything okay?" Bret asks as we turn into the driveway.

"Now, yes, everything is okay now," I say as calmly as possible.

"What was wrong?"

"That is a long story I'd be very unhappy to tell you next time we meet."

Despite the tension, Bret smiles when he asks, "So, there will be a next time?"

"Yes, Bret-of-Flint, there will be a next time," I say when I get out of the car. I walk two steps away, then turn back. I motion for him to roll down the window. "I'm happy to tell you about the car, but *quid pro quo,* which is Latin for 'you show me yours and I'll show you mine.'"

"What do you want to know about me?" he asks.

I kiss him through the open window, then ask, "Who was the dancing girl you were staring at in one of the videos?"

He looks embarrassed as he rolls up the window and backs out of my driveway. I wonder if he'll back away from telling me his truth. It couldn't be as ugly as mine.

"What was Paul doing here?" mom shouts at me when I walk in the door. Dad stands beside her like a pot ready to boil.

"What did he say?" I counter her question with one of my own. Dad frowns, hard.

"He said you were expecting him!" Mom has only got one volume, and it is ten.

"What did you say?" If I keep asking questions, then maybe I won't have to answer one.

"We said you were not home," mom says, still not calming down. "Not that we knew where you were. You can't act like this, Johanna. It's not safe, and it's not healthy."

"He was drunk." Dad says all serious. Unlike my mom, he doesn't need to scream to get me to listen to him since he must know it is his attention and approval that I want.

"I thought you were done with *him*!" Mom adds more volume to a situation that needs none. "I mean you're almost twenty; you should know better. How can you be smart and—"

"And so dumb. I know mom. You've said it before."

"Does he still live in that trailer with his mom? Has he changed at all?"

I think about how Paul promised me he would change and never did even though every day I prayed and hoped I would somehow do or say something that would make the difference.

"I don't want him around again," dad says.

I nod, chew on a thumbnail, and start toward my bedroom, unsure how I'm supposed to keep Paul away when I hear it. In the driveway, the music blares into our house.

Paul's back, and he's brought Springsteen along, trying to coax me out of the house.

Behind Bruce's passionate vocal, I hear Paul's voice, which is more shouting than singing. I rush toward the door and outside. He kicks open the passenger door. I don't climb in as my muscular memory would have me do.

"Paul, what are you doing here again?!" I shout as loud as I can.

He answers by turning up the music so loud that my ears hurt. Inside, I imagine my mother gnashing her teeth and my father balling his fingers into fists.

"You need to leave right now!" I fear for Paul, and I fear for myself.

"I'm not going anywhere until you give me what I want!" Paul shouts back from the car.

I can't imagine that I have anything left he wants; he had taken it all. He owns my past, he's haunting my present, and he's compromising my future with Bret.

Bruce sings, but he's in the background now as Paul's voice grows louder. Paul's not singing; he's screaming the words like he is wounded.

I walk to the car to tell him to turn the music down and leave, but when I get to the car, my knees and confidence betray me as my ears fill with lyrics about being born to run seared into my skull:

I turn around, and my parents are a united front behind the screen door. I reach into the car to turn down the music, but Paul grabs my arm hard. This muscular memory I don't need. I pull away and back away from the car. He restarts the song and we're back in a runaway American dream. "Let go and leave my house now!" If Paul can echo Bruce, I can echo my mom.

"No, Star, I need to see you," Paul pleads. "We were born to run!"

"You need to go now." He answers with a cold-as-ice blue eye stare.

"Joha, please don't turn me away again," Paul says in a begging tone. The door opens and I see my dad starting toward us.

"Paul, please." And it is all coming back to me being with Bruce blaring and our hearts breaking. "You need to leave now, please."

He clicks the player and *"If I Shall Fall Behind"* comes on and I hold back tears.

"Turn it off!" I yell, beg, and plead. "Please, turn it off!".

Memories of the sweet times slam against the sour scene in front of me.

"You, out of here, now!" I hear my dad shout from a shrinking distance.

Paul opens the driver's side door and stumbles out of the car. I grab his arm and try to push him back in the car. He won't move. "Paul, please, Paul."

"No!" I can smell the beer on his breath. "I came for you, Star. I came for you!"

I push him again gently, but he pushes me back, hard. I hit the ground and in an instant my dad is in Paul's face. "You son of a bitch! You keep your hands off my daughter, or I'll beat the crap out of you!" Paul reacts but not as I would have guessed. He breaks out a broad smile.

"Now that's a terroristic threat. You need an anger management class, old man!" Paul half shouts and half slurs. "You're lucky I don't have you arrested for that, but since I'm all in tight with your daughter, I guess I'll let it go, this time." Paul can't stop laughing after his tirade.

I pull myself up off the hard pavement and get between the two of them. "You need to leave now, or I will call the police!" I shout. "Dad, go back inside, I can handle this."

"Then do it!" dad shouts back.

And handle this I know I must. I'm not some high school girl anymore. I need to handle my own problems and none of them are bigger than getting Paul back out of my life.

Paul and dad stare each other down until Paul climbs back in his car. Before I can say another word, Paul revs the engine, turns up the music, and exits loudly to Bruce's "*Badlands.*"

Dad starts inside, so I follow him in the door although there's just about any other place in the world I would rather be. "Why did you let him push you like that?" mom asks.

Dad's face is beet red. "This is unacceptable. I intend to call his father—"

"His dad is dead. His mom, well, she's a mess. He's all alone in the world."

As soon as I get inside, I call Sydney. It is late, so I wake her, but she doesn't seem upset. I think she is delighted in my drama, missing any of her own this summer.

She no more says hello than I tell her the story of Paul's home invasion. She responds with sighs and gasps, then the not unexpected advice to have him arrested.

"I can't do that no matter how much my parents want it."

"Why not?" Sydney asks.

I pause before I confess the ugly truth. "Because that is what they want!"

She sighs again, then asks, "What are you talking about?"

I recount for her my fraught relationship with my parents, in particular regarding Paul. "They wanted him gone from my life, which only made me want him more."

"But what do you want from him now?" she asks, the final Jeopardy question.

I chew on my thumbnail until it bleeds like my heart. "I want to fix him."

Another sigh, then she says, "Jo, you can't fix what is broken beyond repair."

After I hang up from Sydney, I'm at loose ends. I try reading, listening to music—anything but Bruce—scrolling social media, but nothing takes my mind away from Paul.

I know Sydney is right. I had tried to fix Paul before because I refused to believe that anyone is that broken. Now, I can't offer him love or even friendship, but I can offer hope and compassion, two things he's been cheated out of most of his life. I'm in full mind melt down when a text pops up from Bret. I turn away, fearing the worst. While he didn't see the trauma drama at my house, Bret got to see me in full hysteria mode. That's not a good look.

"Just checking to see if you are okay?" he texts.

"Fine." The less I say here the better.

"You seemed weirded out by something." He's on to me. I need protection so I lie.

"I didn't want to face my mom's interrogation about being out with you."

"OK." I hate to lie to Bret, but neither of us can handle my truth right now.

"Despite all that nonsense, I had a great time," I text. "See you soon?"

"As soon as I can." he responds. I don't tell him but that's the wrong answer because soon as I can is not soon enough. We text more about nothing, and it means everything to me.

12 / Bret

"Johanna, you're in Flint!" I say as I gaze across my Goodwill check-out station. I have just five minutes left on my shift. "How did you know I'd be working today?"

She laughs. "I'm a journalism student and reporter. I can get answers from anyone."

"My shift ends in like ten minutes." I don't need to check my phone. I have a straight shot look at a clock in the store, which I stare at endlessly just waiting to be anyplace else.

"I'll be over in the books," she says. "Maybe I can find another Allen Ginsberg tome."

Now it is my turn to laugh. "Good luck with that! I think every other book is by James Patterson rather than geniuses like Steinbeck, Kerouac, or Ginsburg."

"Sounds like Barnes & Noble," she says, then heads off to the book section. She wears a white Detroit Tigers' t-shirt to match her ball cap and a new pair of jeans she fits into nicely.

Engaged for the first time all day, I ring up my last two customers, then close out the register. I head to the back, put away my work vest, then meet her in the book section.

"Do you really want another Ginsburg book?" I ask.

She shrugs. She doesn't seem the hipster type, not that I know that much about her yet. She dresses pretty normal, unlike me, and has a shy-girl vibe.

She picks through the torn paperbacks. "I don't even think they have a poetry section."

"We need a Jellybean!" I say far too loudly for the serious Goodwill bargain hunters.

"What are you talking about?" she asks.

"Let's take a little Flint road trip. You got time?" I ask.

She glances at her phone. "I got like an hour before I need to get home or get yelled at by my mom, again. So why not!"

I don't say that I kind of miss being yelled at by my dad -- at least it was some communication between us. All we have now is a phone and fifteen minutes. "Follow me."

I lead Johanna out to my moldy oldie Metro. "Sorry about the mess. I don't have a lot of company," I say, realizing too late it makes me sound pathetic. Her pity I don't want or need.

"No worries." She doesn't say a word about the backseat filled with empty coffee cups. I open the door, old-school-gentleman style, which elicits a smile. Like her laugh, it's a good one.

The ride to Jellybean Used Books and Records only takes about ten minutes. She doesn't mention the incident where she made me drive around the block, and I let it go as something that is none of my business. Instead, I tell her about the genius of Jellybean as we pull into the small, deserted parking lot. I don't tell her that I had just left Jellybean before I caught Kylee cheating on me with Sean. For a while, I couldn't shop there because of the association.

"Let me buy you something," I say as soon as we enter.

Dennis, the night guy, waves at me. He knows me and my wallet very well.

"I got just the thing." I say.

"Bret, you don't need to buy anything."

"Hell, woman, you braved a trip to Flint. That deserves a reward." I walk her over to the poetry section, and to no surprise, it is still there. *The Outlaw Bible of American Poetry*. I hand it to her. "Ginsburg is here, but so are Tom Waits, Tupac, everybody who matters."

"Springsteen?" she asks, which is odd. She doesn't seem the working-girl Boss-love type.

"Like I said, everybody that matters." She frowns as I try to remove my Chucks from their firm place between my lips. "Sorry about that. I shouldn't knock anyone's musical taste. Well, except on Twitter, where I just rip them. You read any of my stuff?"

"I'm not much on social media. I prefer real media like newspapers."

I let the comment pass and take the book to the register. "I underlined all the good parts."

"What do you mean?" I open the book where it has my name written inside the front cover with my barely discernible Hendricks' scrawl. I pay Dennis and put the book in her hand.

"Next up, The Venus. It's just a few blocks down the road." I almost race to the car, and she joins me in my mad dash. "I don't want to waste a minute of my time with you."

She covers her face like she's hiding a blush. I can't tell if that's a good sign or a bad sign, but I press on and we land on Venus in two minutes.

"Sit back here. It is Elizabeth's section." We head toward a back booth. Seconds later, Elizabeth appears with water, menus, and a black coffee for me. She knows me well.

"Johanna, this is Elizabeth, the queen of the late-night shift."

"Bret, don't call me that," Elizabeth says as she walks away.

"My pal, Alex, used to date her. He even wrote a song about her by that name. But now."

"Now?"

"He's gone, she's here, a sad story, but that's Flint. I am the last man standing."

"Why did you stay?" Johanna asks.

I shrug my shoulders and then pull out my wallet to show it's mostly empty contents. "I didn't have the money or a scholarship to afford to go away. I envy you, Johanna."

I coax another blush from her. "I thought I might get an acting scholarship, but the only people to get free rides out of Southwestern are ball throwers and bouncers. It's a jockarchy."

"That's not a word," she corrects me, but I wave her away.

"That's what Alex and I used to call the water-walking bullies like Dave Hitchings who seemingly got away with most anything they wanted except beating the shit out of someone at the prom," I grimace at the memory, but don't show it. "Oh, wait, that someone was me."

"That sounds terrible." She sounds genuinely concerned, not a faker. Good to know.

"It was two years ago. I don't think about it now." I don't know why I lie to this nice girl. It is rare a day goes by that I don't flash on bad times with Hitchings, good times with Alex, and great times with Kylee.

"You ready to order?" Elizabeth asks.

"I'll have an ounce of—"

"Not now, Bret," Elizabeth cuts me off. She's twenty-one and my pot provider.

We both just order burgers and fries, but as I look across the table, I know what I am hungry for and it's not a burger. As we wait for the meal, I slide over to Johanna's side of the table quite uninvited. "Let me show you all that you missed by not knowing me before this."

We squeeze together as I pull out my phone and run through photos of me acting on stage at Southwestern and me singing with Radio Free Flint. She seems impressed.

"I don't have any photos of me typing up newspaper articles, so my bad," she jokes. "The best I can do is share photos of me and Sydney, both at Columbia and us back in Pontiac. We look like major nerds in our work uniforms: me all dressed up and her in her waitress garb."

We share photos and stories, but mostly laughter, until the food arrives. Between bites, we compare high school experiences and horror stories. Somewhere, we both realize even though she drove fifty miles to meet with me, while we have chemistry, we have little in common. Except one thing that men and women have in common.

"You wanna come back to my house. Nobody's home," I say

She sips her coffee then does a little pretend pout. "Why would I do that?"

I don't know her well enough to know if she's serious or just busting me. "Well, I can think of a few things." Before she can respond, I kiss her on the cheek, then on the mouth. She doesn't resist. We're still lip locked when Elizabeth brings the bill.

"Get a room, Bret," Elizabeth cracks.

I turn to Johanna, then whisper, "I have one in mind."

The Venus isn't far from the house, so it doesn't take long. The free-flowing conversation of before is replaced by awkward silence. I put in the only Radio Free Flint CD to fill the void.

When we get to my house, nobody is home. Mom's at work, Robin's off doing whatever sixteen-year-old girls do, and dad is behind bars. We're a family fractured.

I ask her if she wants a soda since mom won't allow alcohol in the house. She passes and sits on the sofa, not where I thought this evening might be headed. I sit down next to her. She asks about Radio Free Flint, and I have no trouble diving into the past since I have no present with the band. Sean and I never recovered our friendship while Alex is cutting me clean off.

"You're sure nobody is home?" she whispers into my ear.

"Nobody but us, Johanna, nobody but us." And that's my cue to kiss her again. And again. And again. By the time we come up for air, she realizes she is running late, but I keep hold of her hand. "You wanna go into the other room?" I ask.

"I don't need the kitchen." And now I know that she is busting me, but I don't mind.

"I was thinking more of my bedroom," I say softly as I squeeze her hand tighter.

"Not yet," she says in two crushing words.

"No?" I ask. "Why not?"

"I didn't say no, Bret," she says, "I just said, not yet."

After I drive her back to her car and kiss her a strong goodbye, I beeline back to The Venus to conduct some parking lot business with Elizabeth. When I return home, Robin is in the living room but doesn't greet me. I'll always be the weird older brother who embarrasses her with my very being, a point she doesn't mind making the few times we're in the same room.

I don't hear mom in her room, so I head to mine. It is loaded with music posters including the iconic shot of my hero Paul Simonon of the Clash smashing his bass from the cover on *London Calling*. The room used to overflow with classic books and kick-ass music, but I traded most of it in to buy Kylee a Valentine gift, which I never delivered after I caught her going down on Sean. It was the gift of an image that keeps on giving me nightmares to this day.

I open the window, let the gentle summer breeze flow in while the pot smoke flows out. I lie down on the bed and think about Johanna, wondering if I blew things tonight asking her into my bedroom. She's the same age as me, but that doesn't mean she has the same experience as me. Kylee made me an early bloomer, and I've been focused on sex since. I think my lame short-lived theater department romances were derailed by my rushing things, but this thing with Johanna seems different. I take one last hit and then realize Johanna might be the key to unlock the shackles that Kylee has had on my broken heart for two years too long.

13 / Johanna

"So, tell me all about your Flint field trip," Sydney asks. We're in her basement as I am avoiding going home to face the inevitable clash of the titans with my mom for being late.

"It was great, except—"

"Except what?" She is very interested in every aspect of my budding Bret relationship.

"He seems pretty stuck in his past. We looked at all these high school photos, and he just talked about high school stuff. Maybe staying in the same city for college does that. You never really leave your past behind, I guess, if it is all around you."

"Maybe." She moves closer to me as we sit together on an old brown couch.

"But then again, I just mainly showed him pictures of you and me. So, who am I?"

Sydney laughs but not so loud as to wake her mom. It is past midnight, and my mom's going to be pissed at me for being late, but then again, when is she not angry at me about something?

"What's so funny?" I inquire.

"You say he's stuck in the past, but you're the one giving rides to your high school ex."

"Paul is part of my past; he is not part—"

"Of your future, but he is part of your present. What do you plan to do about that?"

I answer with silence as my heart beats faster and sweat breaks out on my brow even though it is cool in Sydney's basement. She moves closer, then asks, "Well?"

"I'm just helping him out, that's all," I say, and I almost believe it.

Sydney laughs way too loud. "He wants back with you. Why can't you see that?"

I consider the possibility and reject it with reservations. If I could have the Paul of the first month, of Christmas week, of the prom, or any of the good times, I would get back with him, but there's also the Paul who controlled me with his words and his violence. Watching him behave as I have the past few weeks, I know that part of Paul is alive and kicking.

"So, you think something is going to happen with this Bret guy?"

I scratch my sweaty forehead and readjust my ball cap, pushing it down over my eyes. "He just seems to rush things; you know what I mean?"

"He's a nineteen-year-old boy. That is what they think about all the time." She laughs again.

It is good my eyes are covered so Syndey can't see them bulge out, then say, "Me, too."

"Really Jo, really?" she asks with more than a hint of sarcasm in her voice.

"I like sex; that's nothing to be ashamed of." A few miles away, I hear mom faint.

"Seems pretty soon, but," Sydney puts her wrist up to her ear and pretends to listen to an invisible watch, "Time is ticking. You have how much longer before you go back to school?"

I think about Bret and sigh at the clock at war against us.

Mom is, of course, waiting at the door for me like I was fourteen and late from school.

I get no more than a few feet in the door when she lets me have it, both barrels. I stand there and take it. I took Paul's verbal abuse, so I take my mother's. Difference was I loved Paul while mom is just a person I share a name and a house with by circumstance, not choice. "I am tired of asking you where you are going and where you have been!" she yells.

"And guess what? I am tired of you asking, so we have at least one thing in common."

"You will not talk to me that way."

Before I respond, I reflect on how I let Paul insult me without recourse. Like Bret, I had high school bullies. One was the boy that I loved, and the other was my own mother.

"Well, are you going to say anything?"

"Yes, good night," I say as I walk past her on my way to my room.

"This isn't over."

I think how the fight for self-respect never is but say nothing.

I go into my room and want to pound my fists on the walls. Even though a bathroom separates me from my parent's room, I don't want to wake dad. He is an innocent, albeit enabling bystander. I am this stress-ball that needs squeezing. It is way too late, but I send the text to Bret anyway. "Please call me!" I know the exclamation point reeks of desperation, but I'm in a state between mom's verbal beatdown and Sydney's truth barrage.

Seconds later he calls. "Johanna, what's wrong?'

Just his voice calms me down. "Nothing, I just wanted to say good night,"

He pauses, probably to look at the late hour. It is past one, and I am one, quite alone.

"I had a good time tonight," he says. I don't know if it's because I woke him up or he finished his transaction with Elizabeth from The Venus, but he sounds groggy. Still, I persist.

"Me too. I'm sorry that I wouldn't go into your—"

"It's okay. We have lots of time."

I glance at my Columbia calendar on the wall where I had been marking off the days until I return. A calendar I stopped marking the day the first time I kissed Bret. A calendar I know is counting down the days until I won't be able to kiss or touch him again.

"I'll be thinking of you tonight, Johanna," Bret says in the sexiest voice possible.

"And I'll be thinking of you," I reply as I put my right hand between my legs.

14 / Bret

I pick up Johanna at the Mall rather than her parents' house. She doesn't tell me about the change in venue, and I don't ask, but I suspect it had to do with whatever happened last time I was in town that caused me to drive in circles

"The park?" I ask when she climbs in.

"Not tonight," she says.

"But I thought that we—"

"Some other place, Bret, some other time."

I frown. I wonder if it's because of the way I look. I should clean-up for her, but I can't bring myself to change my Goodwill employee discount brand: a red bowling shirt with the name "Hank" stitched on it and a torn pair of black jeans. My hair is tinted red and my nails all black to make me color-coordinated if not fashion challenged. I miss the days when I used the theater department costume room as my personal shopping mall. She's dressed in a white

97

button-down and khakis work clothes although she's thrown on her Tiger's cap and her pair of designer sunglasses.

"Then where to?"

"Let's just drive around for a while, ok?" Johanna asks. I nod and start toward the expressway.

"Watch any more of my videos?" I ask her. She nods but says nothing.

"You can't hear the music that good on them," I say. I reach for the CD and put it in. Before she says a word, the genius of Radio Free Flint fills the car. She moves her head to the music, smiles, but says nothing as the music washes over us as we drive. She doesn't give me directions, so we head the only place I know, toward Flint.

We're about halfway there when I notice her look at her phone. "We can head back to Pontiac now," she shouts over the music. "I think it is safe."

"What's there?" I ask, confused but intrigued.

"You'll see," she answers, then turns the music louder. We drive back toward Pontiac with the sounds of my past guiding me toward something I sense is good in the present.

After a drive back to Pontiac well over the legal limit, I pull into the driveway at Johanna's house. I notice the lights are not on. She must notice the same because she says, "Looks like they've given up waiting up for me. Come on inside."

Johanna's right. Her mom or dad are nowhere to be seen We slip quietly up to her room. It is filled with books spilling all over the place coupled with notebooks. There's an overstuffed trophy case and "Honor student" framed certificates on the wall. I see her copy of *Howl* on the bed. The room is smart yet unpretentious like Johanna.

She gently closes the door and grabs onto me. She turns so her back is against the door, and I press against her. She reaches behind and locks the door, then goes over to her computer and turns on some music I don't recognize. She motions for me to be quiet, then returns.

When we don't hear her parents stir, I push her gently against the door. She doesn't push back. Instead, she grabs onto the back of my neck and holds me tight like I was a drowning man.

"Other time is now, other place is here," she whispers.

"Here, really?" I whisper in her ear just before I fall to my knees. She drops her jeans, then clutches my shoulder with her left hand as she puts her right hand over her mouth, so she won't make any noise. Good luck with that.

15 / *Johanna*

I'm up in Flint again, visiting Bret and taking a tour of the battered city seen through his eyes. I wonder if we'll end up at his house like we did last time. Part of me knows being with Bret at my house was dangerous, if delightful. I viewed it as a big 'fuck you' moment to my mom with her being about ten feet away from shattering any last illusions about my innocence.

When we pass by his old high school, Bret tells me stories of how he used to get into trouble for mouthing off to teachers. "I bet you were an overachieving, Honor Society type," he says. I blush big time, which is stupid because there's nothing embarrassing about being smart

We go by a boarded-up Kmart store, and he tells me how his band played there when they were kicked off the school grounds for putting on an alternative music performance for homecoming. He describes an unauthorized concert in the school parking lot, including the abrupt end to it from the school principal, so they moved it to the Kmart. He points out where he set up his make-shift stage. He tells these things in perfect detail like it all happened yesterday. I look at the parking lot closely, and I know. "Park the car," I say. This is the place from the video; this is the story of that dancing girl.

He reclines his seat, and I follow suit. A gearshift separates us again, but our lips come together. I'm trying to get lost in him, but the girl in the video haunts me. I need to know.

"The girl dancing in the video. You couldn't keep your eyes off her. Who is she?"

"Was." Bret says.

"Then who was she?" I hate the genie of jealousy, screaming in my ear.

He takes a deep breath, then squeezes my hand like one of us is on our deathbed. "Kylee. She's gone now, like my friend Alex. She fled Flint for New York, too. She's going to school at Vassar upstate and seems really involved in music and dance. She seems—"

"Stalk much?" I ask.

"It's not like that. I want things to work out for her, but part of me is still angry at how she treated me." He tells me about being cheated on and the heartbreak and humiliation he endured. "But I guess it is true: what doesn't kill us makes us stronger."

I don't tell him how hard it is to keep being strong in the face of Paul's inserting himself back in my life. I regret taking that first call but have no access to a time machine, so I am stuck with the consequences of my action for better or worse but mostly worse it seems. A Paul trait.

"She doesn't matter. You matter, Johanna." He leans over to kiss me, and I try to meet him halfway but the gearshift jams into my side. "All that matters is you."

"I don't know what to say."

"Yes, you do," he says, holding me closer. "You can tell me about the black Firebird in the driveway that day you made me circle the block."

"I don't know where to begin. It started with me saying to Paul, 'I want you to kiss me.' He separated me from my best friend, turned me against my parents, caused my grades to drop, and yet through it all, I loved him."

"So why was his car in your driveway?"

I explain how my simple act of kindness has turned into a full-blown crisis, climaxing that evening with a scene in front of my house that happened after Bret left.

"I wish I would have known before," Bret says. "I would have protected you."

"I need to protect myself, not from Paul, but from thinking about Paul," I say and start to cry again. He pulls me closer, ignoring the gearshift, then oddly starts to laugh.

"What's so funny?" I ask

"Maybe they'll meet each other and destroy each other's lives like they did to us."

"Paul doesn't need destruction," I say. "He needs the one thing I cannot give him."

"Sex?" he asks.

"Forgiveness." I answer.

Bret pulls me closer. "That was the hardest thing I had to do with Kylee – forgive her."

"How could you forgive her?" I just try to imagine the depth of Bret's pain at her cheating on him with his best friend. My heart breaks for him when I think about it.

"I just did. We had this tearful conversation where she burned her diary that recorded her falling out of love with me and in love with Sean. I think the catharsis of that moment helped."

"I tried burning Paul's gifts and mementos of our time together. It helped, but only short-term." The reason that I can't forgive Paul is I don't know how. I can say the words, but they have no meaning behind them, maybe because when Paul says, 'I'm sorry,' I know those are just hollow sounds of half-truth.

"You could start with giving that back." Bret points to the star necklace. I stupidly once told Bret that Paul gave it to me.

I clutch it, then press it against my chest. It is the only good part of Paul I have left. The bruises outside have long since healed, but scars remain. The necklace reminds me of the good, which I want to hang onto even if I know better. Common sense and lost love don't mix.

Bret doesn't say a word. He doesn't argue or force the issue. He is the anti-Paul, and I couldn't be happier until the reality of our situation hits me: I am going back to school, and he is staying here. Nothing can change our direction forward, and I am tired of looking backwards, so I look straight ahead into Bret's eyes. I kiss him with all the madness left in my soul.

16 / Bret

No tour of Flint would be complete with a stop at The Venus. I grab my usual table near the back, and Elizabeth brings up two coffees. When it comes, Johanna, like Becca, ruins it with cream and sugar. I wince and hope she doesn't notice my reaction.

"I am going see my dad in jail tomorrow morning," I tell her.

"That must be so hard." She reaches her hands across the table for me to hold. I don't miss the opportunity. My nails are painted black while her short bitten down ones are free from color.

"You know, you grow up thinking of your parents as these heroes, and then, over time, they turn out to be real people. Flawed, real people."

"Except my mother," Johanna says. "She has never made any mistake except once admitting to a mistake."

I don't say anything about my mom, mainly because she's not really part of my life anymore. We share the same home, but she's always working or sleeping in her room. We exchange texts, rather than talk. Dad is in jail, and in some ways, I guess my mom is, too. "He's getting out soon. I know he'll be sober when he gets out, but can he maintain it is the question."

"Will you need to drive him around because of his DUI?" she asks. I nod.

"I guess between that and your job, you won't be in Pontiac much."

She pulls her hands away, takes off her glasses, and then sits them on the table. Her pools of brown pull me in even if the words I'm going to say will drive a wedge between us.

"I guess not." The restaurant seems to grow silent, or maybe it is because we're talking about the subject we've avoided discussing: the distance between us. She stirs her coffee while I bounce the menu that I know by heart off the table in time to my heartbeat, which grows faster.

"Johanna, we can make this work if we want it bad enough," I finally say.

"I can't handle another heartbreak," she whispers.

I wonder if either one of us can handle another heartbreak as, based on our talk the other night, we're both still getting over one. The only one that matters. The first-love heartbreak.

"It's so complicated, you up here, me down there," she says.

I throw kerosene on the fire. "You soon in New York, me stuck in Flint."

"Like I said, complicated," she says, but that is all she says. She doesn't engage me in the topic that if we're going to be a couple, we're going to have to talk about again and again. Yet we also avoid a deep dive into the subject like somehow that will make it disappear.

I think how Alex and I, with all of our years together, are coming apart to the distance, so how will Johanna with our limited, if intense, history, survive a divide of miles? I decide to challenge her.

"How bad do you want this?" I ask.

She pushes her coffee cup and glasses aside then leans over the table. "Bad."

"And bad is good," I whisper. She rolls her eyes then sighs.

"My parents want to meet you. I guess to make sure you're not crazy," she says.

"When?"

"ASAP."

"Do you believe in us?" I ask.

She puts her glasses back on and reclines in her seat against the worn and torn upholstery that makes up the not-so-fine Venus décor.

"I don't know what to believe," she says. "I was going to come home this summer, work this part-time job, read a lot, and hang out with Sydney. But you, Mr. Bret Hendricks, were not part of the plan, and I do like to plan things. I don't like surprises."

I think about the shock of seeing Kylee with Sean. Surprises are not for me either.

"So, we got some time to figure it out," I say. "The rest of the summer at least."

Johanna smiles at me like she did that first day in the hallway at the courthouse. In that smile shines bright a person of beauty and intelligence and confidence. All I ever wanted.

"I leave end of August," she says, as if I hadn't already checked the Columbia calendar.

I look at my phone. "Well, I guess we don't have much time then after all."

She gives me that look, eyebrow raised, and slightly skeptical, yet also inviting. "Time for what?"

I dart my tongue out of my mouth and lick my lips. She shakes her head and laughs.

As soon as we're in the car, I say, "I got one last thing to show you in Flint."

"It's been quite the exciting tour." Johanna says full of sarcasm.

I put my right arm around her shoulders and steer the Chevy with my left hand. She leans in close, and it feels nice.

"There's something I want you to see." I take Fenton south toward 12th street. It's a quick trip, if not an entirely smart one to be in this part of the city this late at night. I make sure the doors are locked as I guide the car down the alley. At the end of the alley, I turn on my brights. The graffiti filled wall seems bigger than ever before.

"There, underneath it all, you can still see where it reads, 'Bret Lives.'"

"Bret, why did you paint your own name on a cement wall?" she asks, then laughs.

"It reminds me that I can get over anything, so I guess I'm showing it to you now, so you'll know that I'll be okay. If this is just a summer thing, I'll get through it, and so will you."

"So, you brought me to tell me that you'll get over me. What are you saying?"

I slap my hands off my forehead wishing I could pound some sense into myself. "I want this. I want you. I want you for the next hour or the next week or the next month. And when that time is up, I know I'll be okay, but I'll be better because I've known you."

"Next hour?" Johanna asks, then takes off her glasses and turns the car off.

"Next minute?" I ask as she leans over toward me.

"Now," she whispers just before she kisses me.

Bret doesn't just live; Bret thrives.

We leave the wall and return to my house where I determine that no one is home except the two of us. This time, Johanna doesn't suggest we go into the kitchen. After a few lame jokes, I quickly lead her into my bedroom. She doesn't ask about the huge Clash poster, but it gets me excited, explaining about Radio Free Flint's fusion of classic English punk with Detroit funk.

She cuts off the music lecture with kisses on my lips and around my unshaven face.

"What time do you need to be home?" I whisper into her ear.

She glances at her phone. "An hour ago," Johanna says, then laughs. I join her.

"So how about being a little later?" I ask as I point toward my bed.

She hits me with this look she calls 'putting the brow' on someone. A nice nonverbal clue that she's wary for whatever someone is asking of her. "Okay, maybe a little later."

"We don't need to take long," I say, then reach out my hand.

She laughs. "I don't know if I like the sound of that."

"Then how about as long as you want?" I sit down the bed and take off my shirt.

She does the same, then joins me on the bed. We kiss like wildfire as our passion burns.

I'm naked in seconds. It doesn't take her long to join me. I pull a condom from my drawer, but Johanna motions for me to return it. "Not yet," she whispers, and I comply.

17 / Johanna

"Nice to meet you, Bret," mom says. She sounds half sincere. She doesn't offer her hand since they are filled with her caffeine and nicotine addictions.

I smile to myself, knowing that if I wouldn't have kept quiet, mom would have met Bret a few days earlier. I don't think she would believe he was on his knees praying.

"Nice to meet you, too," Bret says, probably trying not to break out in laughter.

Dad does the man-to-man handshake. "So, you're from Flint." His tone is disapproving as if Bret could control where he lived, unless he raced to New York to be with Alex, not that Alex, from what Bret has told me, wants him there. He's not mentioned following me to New York, which is good because despite how great the past weeks have been with us, Bret's not a page in my life planner.

"The vehicle city where they don't build cars anymore." Bret says, then laughs. My out-of-work auto industry mother fails to find this funny. Dad crosses his arms and glares at Bret.

"Don't worry, the auto industry is bouncing back soon," Dad says like he's trying to convince himself. Or maybe trying to sway my decision to return to Columbia to study journalism, and instead going to Michigan Tech and becoming an engineering drone.

"Well, the industry collapsed on my dad," Bret says, then tells the sad story of his father's serial factory unemployment and car wash manager underemployment. Smartly, he doesn't mention that his father's current workplace is the Oakland County Jail.

Dad tries to pep-talk Bret, who smiles politely, but he's not buying a word, I can tell.

"So where are you going this evening?" mom asks.

"Just out" is all the explanation they need from me.

Mom frowns and gulps her late-night coffee cup. The coffee and nicotine pump up her adrenaline, which might explain her volume. It is her controlling tendencies that explain her mood and that I'm living my life on my terms, rather than I hers, that gives birth to her resentment.

"Be back before midnight, Johanna." Dad says, all official sounding.

I nod in agreement even though I have no plans to return at any assigned hour.

Mom frowns again. "You heard your father." They are a two-person wrecking crew.

I nod again, so much so that my neck begins to ache. I put my hand down by my side and Bret takes the cue. Our fingers intertwine as we start out the door. Mom yells her rules at me again, but I'm already gone before they register.

"You wanna smoke?" Bret asks to my surprise. I wonder what he is thinking.

I'm hesitant, knowing the effect substances had on Paul, but I'm also smart enough—and experienced enough—to know that weed doesn't turn you into a ball of anger. Sometimes, I wonder if Paul had been a smoker rather than a drinker if he would have hurt me as bad.

"Sure. You hooked up?" I ask.

"Elizabeth, the queen of the graveyard shift, from The Venus."

I laugh. "One never turns down a queen."

"Where to?" And in an instant, I know where I must be if this thing with Bret is going to be real. I direct him to Pontiac West. I need to close the circle; I need to come fully clean, and it is past time that he did as well. Maybe this illicit inspiration will lead to a long due in-depth and intense conversation. Can we be more intimate in the present without dealing with our pasts?

Bret thankfully doesn't light up in the car while we are driving. We get to the high school parking lot, and it is deserted save for a few cars with people in them probably doing the same thing if not for the same reason. "Park over by that dumpster."

"At Flint Southwestern, the dumpster was called the cafeteria storage unit." Bret says, then takes out a bag of store-bought pot and rolls us a joint.

The term 'storage unit' leads to another memory that cuts me to the quick. The storage unit where Paul would hide and drink while he told me he was working. He stored only deceit.

"You first," I say, but Bret laughs as he holds the unlit joint in his right hand.

"You know that I think women should come first," he says. I blush beet red.

"I won't disagree with that," I flirt back with him, then he hands me the joint. I inhale, but cough like a person with lung cancer. It's been a while since Sydney and I would stall preparing for exams by first examining all the deep truths deep in our souls with weed enlightenment.

"Why here?" Bret asks as I hand him back the joint. He seems to inhale without any problem. It's good that he'll be calm when I summon the storm. If he's going to know me, really know me, then he needs to understand everything about me. That starts tonight.

We smoke the joint down to the nub and use it to light up another one. It doesn't take long before we finish it, and we're laughing about nothing and everything before I bring us down. "There's something I need to tell you about this place."

"Is it haunted?" he asks.

"Sort of. It brings up bad memories of my ex." I'm not Catholic but tonight I will be an exorcist.

He doesn't say a word; he just takes a deeper drag on the new joint and lets me tell the sordid tale. "And here at this dumpster on the night of the Valentine's Day dance,

Paul beat me up. It wasn't the first time, and I am ashamed to say it, it wasn't the last time either."

"Johanna, I don't know what to say."

"You don't have to say anything. It is like that line in the old Beatles song "Yesterday" and how the shadow of the past can hang over a person." I don't tell Bret more details about how I've let Paul worm his way back into my life.

Paul offers me the last hit on the joint, but I wave it away. It served its purpose, taking off enough of the edge to finally admit my truth and sorrow and shame.

"I don't know what to say," Bret repeats like he's stumbling to find the right words.

"I do," I say. "Tell me more about the girl in the video."

"Not much more to say," Bret says. "She destroyed me, Johanna, destroyed me. But I forgave her, and that set me free of her spell over my life. Like I said, she is past tense. Was."

"I don't believe you," I say. Not that I know anything about her, and maybe not that much about Bret, but too much about my own shattered self. Forgiving isn't that easy.

"I believe you keep the past in the rear-view mirror and drive forward straight ahead."

Realizing the pot hasn't loosened his tongue and having admitted my truth but suspect that I've not learned all of this, I tell him we should go. Bret was right. My high school is indeed a haunted place.

Bret drives us from school to a place I recommend: a dirt road by my house where he parks. It is clear what's on his mind and what I have in mine. There's a vacant field not that far away. It's out in the open rather than crammed in the back seat or risking getting caught by my parents. That was a rush at my house with them asleep in the other room, but it was also, I realize now, too big of a risk. I need to be more careful and not have them ruin this relationship with Bret.

"Let's find a clearing," I say. He reaches into the back seat and pulls out a beach blanket. We leave the car and head out for parts and actions unknown but not totally surprising or unwanted. I want that human touch. I am two years and two partners removed from Paul.

We walk out into the open field, and Bret finds a place near an old oak tree. The tree towers over us like some watchful god, but my Sunday school teaching doesn't kick in.

"You're sure you're okay with this?" he asks again, his voice tone tentative.

While I'd prefer another location or situation, I walk a step ahead. He lays out the blanket under the tree. We barely sit down when he is nuzzling up against my neck. I take off my cap and my glasses, which are starting to steam up, and set them gently aside. I hope that gentle is the watchword of the evening. We kiss and roll around on top of each other.

He starts to push up my shirt while I take his off. I bury myself in the soft fur on his chest and listen to his heart pound out a rhythm just for me. He removes my t-shirt. I unsnap my bra, and unlike the aggressive technique of Paul, Marcus, or Roman before him, Bret takes his time and listens to my body as I respond to his soft touches rather than groping. I tousle his hair, then pull the rubber band holding together his ponytail. His long, tinted green hair falls on his shoulders and tickles my nose. I undo his pants, but when I start to pull them down, he stops me.

"No, you first," he whispers as he pulls my jeans down. The backseat of Paul's Firebird had nothing on this beautiful night under the stars and moon. I feel free.

18 / Bret

"There's not much to say" is my weak answer to Johanna's question. Apparently, my 'was' answer about Kylee wasn't good enough even if the sex between us was fantastic.

"You owe me more than that," says everything as we climb back in the car.

I think about how the now fully clothed Johanna bared her naked soul. It is only right that I do the same. "Like I told you before, her name was Kylee."

"And she's some sort of dancer?"

"Among other things," I admit. It is the pot talking as I ramble about Kylee, probably telling Johanna everything she doesn't need to know, but focusing on her cheating. Like her ex- Paul, both seemed to delight in deceit and bullying. Perhaps one day they'll meet in hell.

"So did she come back from Vassar this summer?" Johanna asks with more than a hint of jealousy in her voice.

There's a jealousy giant in me that I learned from hard experience.

"No." I try to hide any tone of disappointment in my voice.

"That's a good school. I looked at it, but they wouldn't give me money, so I picked Columbia," Johanna says. My mind flares like the sun with thoughts of Kylee and Johanna meeting in New York.

"I ended up at U of M Flint because I had the two essential ingredients: a pulse and a checkbook," I crack wise.

Johanna laughs, and I hope it is just not from the pot.

"You in touch with her?" The green slime oozes over Johanna's sexy self.

"You with Paul?" I ask in return.

"Not by my choice, but that's going to change."

"You still think about her, don't you?" Johanna asks, sounding insecure.

I pull her close and whisper in her ear. "No. You're the only thing I think about." She doesn't challenge me, and I wonder why. Does she believe or not believe me?

We sit in silence. I offer to light up the last joint, but she declines by laughing as everything so serious seems funny. We talk more about everything but our past and our future, taking turns between topics to kiss, laugh, and kiss some more.

I'm about to light up when Johanna touches the joint. "You're sure you're good to drive?"

I think about my dad and wonder if anyone said the same thing to him before his DUI. I put away the last joint rather than risking arrest or accident. "Don't worry, Johanna, I'm seriously not seriously fucked up."

She laughs at my double-talk. "I want you to call me, so I know you made it home safe."

I assure her I will, then we start toward her house. I kiss her long and soft before she climbs out of the car and back into her house where I am sure her mother is waiting up once again trying to catch her being late and, in this case, high.

I get back to Flint slower than usual with the music on loud. I turn toward my house, but I don't feel like going home. It's been an epic evening, and I need to end it that way. Instead, I drive over to the Edmonds' house and park outside like some stalker. I wonder if Kylee is home and if so, why wouldn't she call me. Maybe in her mind, I'm just another casualty of her cruelty.

I need to see it again. I make it to 12th street in no time, then head for the alley. There are no other cars around as I park the car and shine the light on the words of "Bret Lives" buried under a cascade of graffiti and gang signs.

And I know it is not right. I get out of the car and head toward the wall. I wish I could wash away all of these other messages and reclaim this real estate as my own. I wish I had some of dad's tools, the few he didn't hock, with me as well. I'll do the best with what I have.

As I walk toward the wall, I reflect for once not on Kylee in this sacred place, but on my wonderful night with Johanna. I think of all I shared with her about my past, about Kylee.

I touch the wall with my right hand, but I pound on it hard with my left until my hand bleeds, but blood isn't enough to do the job like a can of paint could. I take a step back and know somewhere under the veil of paint that the wall still proclaims that "Bret Lives," but I know after my talk with Johanna about Kylee, the V doesn't really belong until I tell Johanna the awful truth that I still think about Kylee most every day. First love, unlike this wall, can't be easily painted over.

19 / *Johanna*

"It's Paul," I tell Sydney, looking at my phone. I had Bret drop me at Sydney's rather than home. We're in the basement at her house. I'm trying to come down from both of my highs.

"Turn off your phone or block him already," Sydney suggests.

"What if there's an emergency and—"

"This is an emergency, and you're in critical condition."

"But what if he's in trouble or needs something?" I ask Sydney.

Sydney sighs loud enough to wake the dead. "He is trouble, and he does need something. He needs you, Jo." She takes the phone from my hand and looks over the roster of his stalking me: ten missed calls and twenty unanswered texts, all just in an hour.

"You'll thank me for this," she says, then dramatically turns my phone off.

"I could have used you in high school to take charge of my life," I joke. Sydney, who loves to laugh, doesn't make a sound. Instead, she hits me with a serious frown.

"No one is gonna take charge of your life unless you let them, like Paul, maybe like Bret." She hands me back my useless phone. I resist the urge to turn it back on.

"It's not like that with Bret!" I protest. I scoot away from her on the couch.

"Then how is it? You've been all shy with the details."

"It's personal." I turn up the volume on the TV. Stupid comic book heroes do stupid stuff on the stupid big screen. "It's not like you shared everything about Gan with me?"

"We fucked. He cheated. Goodbye loser. There's the six-word version of it," she says matter of fact like it was just something that happened to her without a lasting effect.

I want to protest my innocence. "We'd done everything but have intercourse."

"And why is that?"

"It hasn't been the right time or place."

Sydney shakes her head. "You'll figure it out, Johanna."

"I mean, this is so different," I confess. "I mean with Paul, it was harsh and fast, sometimes fueled by rage or alcohol, never any tenderness, but Bret is different."

"Different is good. I wish I could go back and tell all my high school boyfriends that."

I consider her remark. "Maybe so," I say soft as Bret's touch.

"You still think about Paul, don't you?" Sydney turns to face me. She grabs my shoulders and shakes me like I was knocked out, and she was trying to revive me. "Even when the two—"

"He was my first love. I can't change that." I start to cry.

"But you can change how you feel about him now. How is that?"

"I feel sorry for him. I can't help it, but I can't forget everything between us."

"You should remember all the stuff between you, like when he hit you"

When I don't answer, Sydney grabs my hands and squeezes them hard. "You can't move on until you forget him, and you can't do that until you do the hard thing."

"What is that?" I ask.

Sydney stares me down like I was her worst enemy. "Forgive him."

"I can't talk long," I tell Paul as I walk up the stairs at Sydney's house and away from her well-intentioned if uninformed opinions on how to run my life. She may be my best friend now, but she's only known me for a year, so she can't truly understand what Paul meant to me.

"I need to see you, Star," Paul says, well slurs as he's obviously drunk.

"Paul, that's not possible. You know that."

"Why not?" He asks like he really doesn't know or maybe doesn't care.

"My parents want you arrested."

Paul laughs, way too loud. I wonder where he is. Is he Firebirding, risking another DUI? Maybe back in the mini-storage unit doing his drinking in secret? Or maybe at his trailer, him in his room, fueling his addiction, his mom watching con men on TV fueling hers. "Go ahead and have me arrested. See if I care."

"You don't mean that Paul." I'm outside Sydney's house under a full moon.

"Why not, Star? Without you, I am nothing." It all came back to me; the very same sympathy ploy played the night of our final breakup. I may not be wiser, but I am older and know enough not to repeat my mistakes, so I say nothing.

"I might as well be in jail if I can't be with you." The slurring gets worse.

"Stop talking this way." I am not flattered but frightened.

"There's been no one but you."

I can't let his lies go on. It is too much for me. "What about Allison? What about Sarah?"

"They meant nothing to me." He says it almost with pride rather than with shame.

"I know about Sarah," I hiss, my anger at him and myself for staying on the phone with him, rising. "I saw the black-eye that day at my graduation party."

He says nothing. He doesn't deny it or explain it. He just ignores it.

"If you keep on with this behavior, you will end up in jail. I don't want to see that."

"I'm in jail without you, Star."

I shake my head in wonder. "You're being overdramatic."

He doesn't deny that either, but that's another page from his playbook. After I left Paul, I read about abusive relationships, and it is almost as though all of these guys operate off the same set of plans: find the insecure girl, separate her from her friends, get her to have sympathy for you, then take control of her life through emotional manipulation coupled with violence. That's what Paul was really about, control, and it is what he wanted to do to me then and now. His own life is spinning out of control, so he wants to take control of someone else. It won't be me again.

"No, Star, I'm being real. I just want you to know I'm telling the truth."

"No, Paul, you are not telling the truth. I don't even think you know what that is."

He goes mute again when confronted with the truth about his lies. "Johanna, I still love you," he says. I don't know if I believe him or not. I believe he loves me, but I don't believe he knows what those words mean either since he can't back them up with actions.

A cool breeze blows, and I shiver. I stand in my best friend's backyard, talking to a ghost. It might as well be

Halloween rather than close to the 4th of July. "Are you there?" he asks.

I consider the question. I weigh my options, and then answer "No" just before I hang up the phone. I start inside, ready to tell Sydney every detail except Paul telling me he still loves me because I hate myself for still having any feelings for him when my phone rings. Bret.

"I wanted to let you know I made it home safe and sound," he says clearly.

"I was worried," I admit and also more than a little feeling guilty about talking to Paul.

"I wish I was there, Johanna. I wish I could see more of you. I want all of you."

"Soon, Bret." But I wonder, can I truly give myself to Bret if still chained to Paul?

"Is that a promise Johanna?" he asks in a tone that washes away all of my doubts.

"It is not a promise," I whisper. "It is a spoiler."

20 / Bret

"How are you doing?" I speak into the black phone. Dad stares from behind the glass.

"Okay, I guess," but his appearance says different. He looks like shit in that orange jumpsuit unform. He's got forty days left, and I'm not sure he's going to make it. I had avoided coming back to visit, but mom insisted. I never could turn down anything she asked of me, so here I am on Saturday morning after waiting an hour in line, sitting with the families of other criminals trying to have a conversation through a phone and a plexiglass barrier. I think that day he got sentenced might have been one of the worst days of his life, but it led to my meeting Johanna, which made it one of the best days of my life. My life is full of doubled-edged swords.

"You still working?" dad finally asks, trying to pretend interest in me for once.

"Over twenty hours a week most weeks."

"That will make a man out of you." Despite Kylee and later Becca, my dad still thinks I'm gay. If he had been a fly in my life the last month, he would change his conviction fast.

"I met someone." He doesn't ridicule me this time for it, so I gush about Johanna. He seems unimpressed, especially when I start talking about her scholarship to Columbia. I talk so much I used up most of our time.

"Ivy League assholes think they are better than everyone."

I insist that dad is wrong, but that's not a position he's ever willing to change. "She's not like that. Sure, she's smart, but she's also sexy and fun to be around."

"Sex makes you pussy stupid. It did me and look what I got. Cameron, who I had at age eighteen, doesn't talk to us. I got two other kids who can't stand me plus a wife who is always a day away from leaving me. Now I got three hots and a cot. It is almost an improvement."

"I don't hate you. I love you." The words are mumbled since they are almost new to me.

He grunts since he can't return with genuine emotion other than anger. "That is never how you acted, and from what you told me, you were some kind of actor."

"If you ever would have gone to my plays, you would have seen me."

He stares me down in full-out fury. I don't know if it is directed outward or inward. I'll never know because other than that one night after Kylee broke my life, he's never confided in me. I learned his father was a son of a bitch, so he grew up the same. I'm not sure what that says about my prospect as a one-day dad. I'm about to launch into it when I hear the terrible words.

"Time's up!" The oversize guard yells. I reach out my hand and touch the glass to try to make a human connection even through a barrier, but dad just walks away with his back to me.

It takes four tries, but I finally reach Alex by text. I guess he's feeling put out because the first line of his text is "What is it???" I question his use of three question marks, but I proceed.

"Can I call?"

"Busy."

"Later?"

"Got a gig."

"Where?"

"U wouldn't know it."

"OK." I recoil from the text slap across the face.

"You want something???"

Another three-question-mark slap. I feel beat up and bruised by his attitude toward me. How could two people who shared so much for so long be so far apart in such a short time?

"I got a new girlfriend."

"OK"

His enthusiasm knows bounds.

"Can I call tomorrow? I want to tell you about her. Texts won't do."

"Busy."

And that word breaks me. It reminds me of all the times I tried to get dad to come to one of my plays, and the one word "busy" was just another hammer on my nail head. Busy wasn't a situation, but an attitude of utter indifference. Busy was one word for "fuck you, Bret."

"Never mind."

"OK."

How could he not care? I shared with him every detail about Kylee, probably ones he didn't need to know, but now, he's a one-word metronome.

"Bret?"

"What."

"I don't have time for this."

"For what."

"I need to focus on now, not then. Not you."

"Seriously."

"Lose my number."

Death by text. I never thought it would happen to me, especially from Alex. Alex, my friend, confident, bandmate, soulmate, and now a nothing man.

I say nothing since words, even short ones, don't seem to matter. I feel cut off from my past, so I look for it the only way I can find it. I lose Alex and desperately reach out to Kylee. As always, she doesn't respond. I could wait days or weeks or months or even a year as it has been, and she's never responded to a single message. She won't block me, which seems out of spite for her to show me what a great time she is having away from Flint while I'm stuck here.

My dad doesn't need me, and my best friend doesn't want me. It is time to cut ties with my past, so I need to make a fateful attempt to sever my only remaining connection to Kylee.

"Why Bret, what a pleasant surprise!" Kylee's mom says when she greets me at the front door. Her father, three inches shorter than his wife, stands beside her. They are both beaming.

"Come in, come in," Kylee's father beckons me into their house. It's been two years, but it looks the same: stuffed with books, rooms covered with cat hair, and an organized mess of their varied interests. He's a history professor at U of M-Flint while she's a professional charity machine. My mom with her low-wage retail jobs is light years away from the Edmunds.

"Would you like something to drink?" Kylee's father says, then starts rattling off his wine list. When he takes a break, I let him know I'm fine. My dad's a great example of why I should never drink even a drop. "Well, to what do we owe this pleasure?"

"I need to get a message to Kylee."

They look at each other, then back at me. "Is everything ok?" Kylee's mom asks.

"Couldn't be better." It feels weird to lie to such nice people.

"We don't hear from her much. She's awfully busy down in the city this summer," Kylee's dad says. I can easily hear the pride in his voice at his daughter's success.

"I just want to let her know that I forgive her." They again look at each other, quite confused and obviously shielded from the emotional tsunami of their daughter. Chad, me, Sean, who knows how many others. "I forgave her before, but she needs to know I still feel that way."

"I know you had a bad breakup with her. Is that what this is about?" her mom asks. "She was quite the hell fire back in high school. We didn't help with that."

I don't answer, but probably enabling your high school senior daughter to have sex with her boyfriend—wait, plural that—probably wasn't such a good idea.

"But she's doing better now. She says she has a new boyfriend, but she won't tell us anything about him. It just takes some people more time to mature than others."

"Well, I hope she is happy. If it matters, tell her that I'm happy, too."

"You know, Bret," Kylee's mom says. "She did love you. She just didn't know how."

Like some movie montage, images of my time with Kylee flash in my brain. But it is one of the movies with scenes that lodge in your brain like some earworm that you can never escape.

"When you talk to her, just tell her that I'll leave her alone." I think not of Kylee, but of Johanna, haunted and harassed by her ex. I don't want to be that guy, hanging on to yesterday, except despite all my best efforts, I am that guy, just not the extreme. If anything, visiting Kylee's parents was the wrong move because it reminded me too much of what I was missing.

We chat some more, but there's nothing much to say. Dr. Edmunds invites me to take a class with him, not knowing that his daughter already taught me everything I needed to know, except she remains a living, breathing history out of reach. I wonder if she'll ever be out of mind.

I exit the Edmonds house as I did so many times before, but this time, I don't look back.

21 / *Johanna*

Over fattening lattes, I finally tell Sydney the skinny on what happened with Bret in the field in probably far too much detail. I hope to relive every minute of it again soon.

"So did you?' She's all smiles. I nod, then blush.

It is weird to talk about this with anyone, even a friend like Sydney, and even more so to do so in public in the middle of a Starbucks. I move the conversation to something less personal, talking how Bret and I don't have a lot in common, yet there is a connection between us.

"He sounds like a great guy. When can I meet him?" Sydney asks eagerly.

"I don't know if you should."

She pouts. "I thought we were friends."

"It's only a summer thing. No sense getting invested in it, or him." I'm sad when I say the words, not sure if I believe them. Bret, or any boy, wasn't in my plans, but now he's front and center and has taken hold of my heart even if Paul beats like a loud drum in the background.

"That is probably best," Sydney says.

"Long-distance relationships don't work, you know that?" Sydney's long-distance relationship with her high school beau lasted all of a month after she moved to New York. I broke up with Marcus before I left for Columbia as a precaution against missing him. It was pulling off the band-aid fast rather than slow. "It is too complicated with Paul in the picture."

"You need to do something about him!"

"What, have him arrested? Have him go to jail? Why would I ruin his life?"

"Maybe because he nearly ruined yours."

I shake my head vigorously. "No, I ruined my life. I chose to stay with him after he abused me. I need to own that. It's not all on him. I let him treat me like that."

Sydney laughs like someone does after you say something funny, but stupid. "Listen to yourself. You are still making excuses. He was the problem. Hell, he is still the problem."

I know she's right, but I can't say the words or admit it to myself. I blame the victim.

"Look, who am I to give advice, little—or rather not so little anymore—loveless me."

Even with her Pontiac-inspired weight gain, which is obvious in her face, Sydney is a beautiful girl, so I start to pressure her about being alone when she doesn't need to be.

"I don't need anyone." She runs her finger through her hair and smiles.

"I don't need anyone either," I insist but feel bad about lying to my new best friend.

She scoffs. "Really, Jo, do you really think that? I mean, you stayed with Paul through terrible times. You stayed with Marcus because it was easier than breaking up with him, and you stayed with Roman until he cheated on you. For someone telling me that you don't need someone, you do a poor job of showing me that. Maybe you should rethink your position."

I don't argue with her because I know she's right, and I hate it.

"Look, you're too smart to know that's not the case. I thought maybe this summer you would realize that, but I guess I was wrong. You do it your way, and I'll do it mine."

"I don't need Bret," I admit. "But I want to be with him."

"No, what you want is not to be alone, which is why you stayed with Paul."

Her truth chills the conversation colder than my latte. I finish quickly then step outside. That's what I need to do with Bret: finish it quickly and then step outside my comfort zone and be alone. Next to the cigarette smokers, I decide to light the fire to burn down my summer.

I tell Bret that I'm busy when he wants to drive down to see me. He's not buying it.

"Look, you're going back to Columbia soon, so we don't have much time," he says.

"I know, Bret. It is complicated, but I just can't see you tonight."

"Will I get the same answer tomorrow night?" he asks, sensing my serious tone.

I chew on my fingernails. They're at the quick. "Yes."

"Did I do something wrong?" he asks, sounding wounded, and I'm to blame.

"No, Bret, I did. I let you in. I'm going back to school. There's a shelf date on this, and maybe we can avoid serious heartbreak by ending it now before we get even deeper."

"So, this is a pre-emptive breakup?" Bret asks. I want to laugh at the terminology, but I hold it in. I need to hold myself together. Sydney's right. I'm wrong, and this needs to be done.

"I guess so," I answer.

There's a long pause. There's plenty of noise between Flint and Pontiac, but I can hear none of it. I only hear my heart beating. "I got a friend in NYC, Alex. Maybe—" Bret says.

"Maybe what?"

More silence from me other than a creeping sense of dread. "Maybe I could move out there, and then, this summer thing wouldn't have to end."

My mind bounces in two directions, from loving this idea to hating it. Is Bret reaching out for me or is he grabbing onto me like Paul? Everything compares to Paul.

"Bret, I barely know you."

He laughs. "You know enough. I wouldn't ever treat you like Paul did. I would never hurt you or harm you. I would never break your heart."

"Then I will break yours. Don't call me again, please."

By the time he hangs up the phone, I'm already in tears. Tears have a taste, and these taste of heartbreak. I want to call him, take it back, but I pull myself together. I will be strong.

22 / *Bret*

As soon as I hang up the phone, I know what I need to do and where I need to go. I tell my manager that I'm headed to break, which makes sense as I feel broken.

I'm in my car in a minute and at the hardware store in five. I buy what I need, then rip down the highway, getting off at Grand Traverse. I turn on 12th then down the alley and drive to the dead end. I get out of my car, go to the trunk, and open it. I pull out my tools.

Like I did years before, I work with purpose and passion. In less than half an hour, I have covered the old graffiti and replaced it with my own new message: "Bret Will Live Again."

I snap a photo, send it to Johanna, and then drive away, wondering if, like before, I can make my bold statement real.

I head back to work in a black t-shirt and blue jeans covered with specks of paint. My manager looks at his watch, grumbles, but doesn't say a word. I focus on the work, greeting customers, ringing up sales, and wondering why on earth people are buying half of what they have in their cart. Don't they know most of this merchandise comes from dead people? They are walking around in the clothes of a ghost.

Just like me.

As soon as I get out of work, I head home to change and shower. Mom's home for once. She used to be the perfect empathy machine, but dad's drinking, arrest, and imprisonment have stripped the gears of her emotional output. She walks through the day, working and going about her business, but with no passion or purpose. Like a ghost.

Just like me.

I want to reach out to Alex, but he shut that window on my fingers. It's up to Becca. She agrees, quite reluctantly it sounds like, to meet me at The Venus for a late-night coffee. While Alex is probably laughing with his new friends at some hipster hang-out in Soho, I'm left to the black-and-white world of Flint and ugly puke green décor of The Venus. It is open twenty-two hours a day. I don't know what they do during those two closed hours, but as Elizabeth has pointed out more than once, it is certainly not clean.

We order, small talk about nothing, then I cut into the meat of the sandwich.

"So, this girl I was seeing from Pontiac broke up with me, just like that."

Becca doesn't look surprised. I'd told her about Johanna, but light on the details.

Elizabeth brings us water, coffee, and menus. I smile, but my attention is solely on Becca.

"That's just wrong," Becca says. I nod in agreement. "I mean, you don't break up with someone just to break up with them. It is stupid."

"That's what I don't get because she seems so smart."

Becca laughs. "Matters of the heart have very little to do with intelligence."

"Then what does it have to do with?"

Now Becca sighs. "If we understood that, maybe we'd still be together."

I don't argue with her. When Becca and I broke up, it was for an unstated reason: I wasn't over Kylee. I'm still not over her, and like a childhood injury that leaves a scar, I never will be no matter how much I say it. Johanna made me, if only for a short time, forget the Kylee corkscrew in my heart.

"So, what are you going to do?" she asks.

"What can I do?" I ask as Elizabeth comes by with coffee. Becca starts pouring in sugar. I want the bitterness of the bean in my mouth.

"I can't tell you that. You're going to have to figure that out yourself," is her less-than-helpful response. She seems really to care, and I regret not being kinder to her. She's probably luckier to be my friend than my girlfriend.

"Don't go to some big, stupid, romantic gesture," Becca says. "If you believe the movies, that's the answer, but it really just makes everything worse."

I tell Becca about sending Johanna the 'Bret Will Live Again' photo. "Yes, Bret, like that."

"I guess I need to fight for her, like I tried to do with Kylee and then maybe—"

She cuts me off. "Maybe you should get over Kylee first, then go after this girl."

There's no sense lying to Becca because she knows better. So, do I. I think of the serenity prayer taped up on the wall of my dad's garage. I know there's nothing I can do to change my past or my present with Kylee, so I must learn to accept it. I have that wisdom, but with Johanna, I don't know if I have the courage to change things. I am the cowardly lion who has too big of a heart and isn't sure sometimes if my brain even works concerning women.

"You still think about Kylee every day? You still stalk her on social media?" Becca asks. I can't say no, so I just drink my black coffee. "You still in love with her?"

I flash for once not on Kylee, but on the black Firebird in Johanna's driveway. I wonder if I asked her the same questions about Paul how she would answer. It hits me: both of us are too stuck in our past to enjoy our present, let alone think about a future. The past haunts Johanna like a ghost.

Just like me.

23 / *Johanna*

As I'm leaving work, I hear Paul's voice. "Joha, look, let me explain."

I grab the keys out of my purse in case I need a weapon if he is the drunk-and-dangerous Paul from the other day at my house. I keep walking to my car, wondering how I can continue to live under this scary shadow hanging over me and what it will take to end it once and for all.

"Look, I'm sorry about the other day, really!" He's shouting because I'm not turning around again. I can't whiplash myself through Paul's emotional high and lows, not again.

I don't answer, so he rants on. "It was a one-time thing. I got drunk. I was stupid!"

I remember how Paul always said his drinking was a one-time thing, but it was a trait passed down from father to son, kind of like his fucked-up relationship with women.

I finally turn to face him down. "Look, if it happens again, I'll call the police, and I'm sure that will violate your probation. I don't want to send you to jail, but you have me in one. I can't answer my phone without flinching. I can't leave work with worrying you'll be here, like now."

"Why won't you forgive me?" Paul asks in his best pleading voice.

Those are the trigger words. I take a step toward him. "Forgive you! For what sin? For hitting me? For lying to me? For stalking me? For making me bitter? For which of these?"

"Look, it's not my fault. I told you about my dad and how he—"

"You can't do that Paul, not again, not anymore. You can't keep coming back with the same excuses and expect me to have some different response. I'm sorry about your past, but you can't keep using it as your excuse. Maybe if you admitted what you did was wrong, then—"

He pokes his finger at me like a sword. "But my dad—"

"Your dad is dead, Paul. He left you first, and then he died. I can't imagine how much that must have hurt, but it doesn't excuse your behavior, which is why I can't forgive you. If you really want my forgiveness, then you admit you are responsible for these bruises on my heart."

I wait for the explosion at the mention of his father, but it doesn't come. Instead, he comes closer to me, and I can hear him crying. "Look, Joha, I'm just all messed up inside."

"I know Paul, I know." He wants me to comfort him, but it's a rat trap I know.

Like he used his words to manipulate me before, now, he uses his tears. Nothing changes.

"I'm sorry. I have to go."

He reaches for my arm, but I pull away. "Really this time everything will be different."

"I know it will because I am different," I say. "Leave me alone or else."

Paul walks past me and gets to my car before I can. He starts pounding on the hood. "Why won't you forgive me?"

"I can't, Paul. If I forgive you, then you won't take responsibility for your actions, not just what you did to me, Sarah, and that girl Allison, but what you will do to others. You keep making excuses, so I can't forgive you until you own up to what you did and to who you are."

"What I am is nothing, Joha. I am nothing without you."

I open the car door and climb inside. Paul bangs on the hood more. I let it play out until I see his hands are bleeding, and he finally stops. I drive off all alone into a night without stars.

I glance at my phone and think of another night without Bret. I roll down the window and watch the Michigan landscape pass me by. With each mile, I stop myself from calling Bret. I got myself into this situation with a bad snap judgement, but now I must figure out a way to get back into this life. For a long time when I was without

Paul, I felt like I was nothing. Without Bret, I am something: heartbroken.

24 / Bret

One good thing about dad not being home is that I can go out to the garage with my bass and my amp, then crank up the volume. When I was just learning in 7th grade, I played every day. Then with Radio Free Flint, we rehearsed every day as a group, but I also practiced on my own every night. During all of this, dad was less than supportive like most of my pursuits.

I put my fingers against the tight strings and press down hard. It has been almost one year since I've played, yet it comes back quickly. I hear Alex's songs, like *"Throw the Lions to the Christians"* in my ear like he just wrote them yesterday. I zing through lots of old Radio Free Flint tunes, then dig deep into the sound files in my head to shuffle through the stuff from when I really learned how to play. Not the school jazz-band stuff I did freshman year, but the deep bass sound of English punk and all sorts of funk, both of which Alex turned me onto when we met. I blow through the best of the Clash, ending with the booming bass line of *"Death or Glory."*

I pick up the phone to call Alex since the music pulls me to him but decide I don't need more rejection. He doesn't answer most calls, and my texts go unreturned. He hasn't blocked me yet, but it is only a matter of time. I'd like to tell him about Johanna, both the good and the bad, but that's not his role anymore. I've yet to recast the supportive best-friend character in my life play. Becca's a nice stand-in, but she's got her own life, and while she listens to my whine without cheese, she must be growing tired of me singing the Bret Hendricks love-sick blues.

I punch out more Clash until Robin starts yelling from inside the house to turn the music down, much like my dad used to say, except it was the "Goddamn racket" when he wanted to silence me. Silence is the last thing I need right now. I can't be alone with my thoughts and visions of Johanna. I call the Oakland County Jail and learn about evening visiting hours. I'm in luck—or maybe not, depending upon dad's mood—since I can visit tonight. I play a little more, but it doesn't help. The boom of the bass just adds to the rattling in my chest and the headache creeping up my spine. A night of crying will do that. I have a heartbreak hangover.

"So, I got dumped," I tell dad through the phone and plexiglass combo that is our life.

"Again?" I don't know if he meant it as an insult, but it sure sounded like one.

"She's going away to school," I start and then tell him the sad story. He doesn't react at all. It is like he is not listening. It is like all those years when he ignored me except to yell.

"Didn't that Kylee girl teach you anything?" he finally asks. He has no idea how much, in good ways and bad. "These teenage girls, they don't know what they want half the time."

"I know what I want," I say in defiance of both him and Johanna.

"Who says you get what you want?" Dad points to the walls around him. This all sounds very familiar to lectures on life he gave me back when I wasn't hearing his words, just his tone. Our conversation is a two-year-old tape loop with neither of us listening or learning.

"Nobody told me that, dad. I know that you don't get what you want."

"You gonna fight for her or get your ass handed to you again?" dad asks.

My getting beat up by Hitchings is something I would rather forget, but I sense that dad never will. It's yet another failed mark in his school-of-hard-knocks gradebook.

"Yes, but I don't know how to do that other than ask her to change her mind."

Dad laughs, not with me, but at me. "Why should she do that?"

"Do what?"

"Change her mind. You better accept you can't change a woman's mind."

I want to ask dad how he got so cynical, but I just remember him talking about his own father being such a hard ass. It's all he knows, so why I should expect any difference now just because for once we broke through this angry-father, stubborn-son routine we had down pat?

"I believe anyone can have their mind changed," I say with utter conviction.

Dad scoffs like my words don't even deserve comment.

"You did. You changed your mind about me at least for a while."

Dad won't look at me because then he'd have to remember when he wasn't deaf and blind to me, remember when he was, for one evening, as good an empathy machine as mom.

"Well, good luck with that girl. You're going to need it."

I think about the difference between need and want and realize Johanna is both. If I can't change her mind, I need to find someone who can. I need the National Coney Island in Pontiac.

I find the tables that Johanna's friend, Sydney, seems to be handling and sit myself right in the middle. When she comes back with an order for the table next to me, she notices me right away wearing my 'Made in Flint' black t-shirt. "Bret, right?"

I flip my pony tail up and kick out my green Chucks for her to see. "You noticed."

"What are you doing here?" She doesn't sound happy to see me.

I pull the classic question-with-a-question move. "When is your shift over?"

"Not for an hour." She's got her hands on her hips and a pissed off look on her face.

"I guess I'll have a coffee then with lots of refills."

She stares hard at me. "I can't help you if that is what you're here for."

"You can't even listen to what I have to say?" I ask.

"I don't have time, and it is not my problem." Her angry mood matches her red hair.

Before I can respond, she is called away to the kitchen when another one of her orders comes up. I pull out my Sharpie and turn over the paper placemat. I write bullet points of all the things I want to say to Johanna via Sydney. Dad was wrong – I can and will change her mind.

I'm deep into the work when Sydney drops off my coffee without a word. The next refills come without comment as my list grows, but then I edit it down to a reasonable number.

- If it isn't broke, why fix it?
- I'm willing to risk heartbreak, so why aren't you?
- If you don't want to get hurt, why not just stay in your room?
- Can we focus on today, not yesterday or tomorrow since we can't change them?

The last one I circle twice: once for Kylee, once for Paul. The ghosts of relationships past.

I check my phone. No messages from Alex, no surprise; none from Johanna, big disappointment, but not anger, just sadness. A deep sadness that I feel in my bones. A sadness I can't shake. A sadness that feels like death visited. A sadness that only Johanna can heal.

"Anything else?" Sydney stops by just before the end of her shift. She speaks with way too much attitude. Maybe she just resents me taking up a table, or maybe Johanna has told her terrible lies about me as a reason for the breakup rather than the truth: it wasn't my fault.

"So, you won't talk to me?"

She dramatically rips off the bill and hands it to me as her answer.

I take cash out of my pocket and put it on the table. "Here's for the coffee."

She nods, takes the money, and frowns. I hand her the marked-up placement.

"What is this?" she asks, looking none too pleased.

"Here's my tip," I say as I stand. "Be a good friend and give this to Johanna."

25 / *Johanna*

"I'm sorry," is all I can say when Sydney shows up at my door just after ten o'clock with a piece of paper in her hand and her story about Bret. "I didn't want you dragged into this."

"I didn't even know if I should give this to you," Sydney says as I let her inside. We head upstairs to my room. Mom waves at Sydney, smiles, no doubt happy that it is not Bret or Paul in her house. If she knew what Paul did the other day, she'd want him back in jail. If she knew what Bret did to me in her house, she'd never forgive either of us.

We go up to my room. I close the door make makes me think about Bret. I remember me pressed up against the door with my hand over my mouth and his mouth buried between my legs.

I take the paper in my hand. "I don't know if you should give it to me either."

"I can understand if you don't want to read it."

"That's the hard part. I do want to read it."

"So, what happened to that whole 'I don't need Bret or anyone stance?'"

I motion for Sydney to sit on the bed. I sit down next to her. I grab her hand but say nothing. I feel no matter what I say it is going to come out wrong. I do my best to read Bret's messy handwriting, sighing and crying along the way. The paper is damp by the time I am done.

"Did you read it?" I ask.

She shakes her head, but says nothing

"What do you think I should do?"

She shrugs her shoulders. "I don't get to say. It's not my life."

"But you told me to break up with him!"

Sydney gets off the bed. "I never said such a thing. I told you that it was your fear of being alone as the reason you stayed with Paul and probably the same reason you are with Bret."

"I'm not afraid to be alone. I just don't like it, that's all."

She laughs at me. "How will you know unless you try it?"

I don't argue with her because she is mostly right. I started seeing Marcus right after Paul more to heal my hurt than anything else. Same with Roman when I moved to Columbia. Between Roman and Bret—all of four months— is the longest I have gone without a boyfriend since I turned sixteen and my mom allowed me to date because I didn't want –as Bret wrote – to stay in my room.

"Just because you decided that you didn't want a boyfriend, don't tell—"

"No, you don't get to make this about me. This is about you and your choices."

"I guess it is easy to decide when I'm sitting with you to support me," I say. "But it is hard to hold onto that choice when I'm alone at night. When the phone doesn't ring. When the texts and pictures don't come. When I know the morning will be as lonely as the night."

"I know it is not easy." She walks back to the bed, then sits down next to me again.

I bury my head in her shoulder. "I just miss him."

She pulls me closer. "Why?"

"Why do I miss him?" I am startled by the question. "He's smart and he's funny and—"

"And he goes down on you, right?" I'm glad she can't see my smile when I'm supposed to be feeling so miserable, but I can't resist that muscular memory.

"That's not the only reason."

"You let Paul bully you one way, and then Bret bully you another way. I don't get it."

"Bret's not a bully."

Sydney laughs. She's having quite the comic evening at my expense. "He uses his body to control you and make you do what he wants. If that is not a bully, I don't know what is."

I pull my head from her shoulder and walk over to my door. I lean my back against it, and I remember not just here but his house and in the field. My body remembers, and it aches.

"So that means what this really is about is the same thing everything is about – Paul."

"You have no idea what Paul did to me," I say. "I told you everything, but I don't think I can ever express the totality of our fucked-up relationship. It was everything right and everything wrong you can have when you're a sixteen-year-old girl. It was true love for the wrong person."

"You were in over your head," she says, and at least she doesn't laugh again.

"But I'm not now," I reassure her. "I know more. I'm stronger, or at least I thought I was. Shakespeare was right about better loved and lost, than not loved at all."

"Shakespeare never met Paul," Sydney snaps.

"This is about Bret."

"Jo, I hate to sound like your mom, but for someone as smart as you, it is amazing how ignorant you are about this. Until you really move on, it will always be about Paul."

"Bret is the sweetness to take the bitterness of Paul out of my mouth." As the words leave my lips, I know I've spoken a truth that trumps everything I said before, even anything on Bret's list of reasons we should get back together. "I think I made a huge mistake breaking up with Bret."

We talk a little more, but it's clear to Sydney that I've changed my mind. She doesn't bash me or shame me. She's there for me, which is all I need in a friend. As soon as she's out the door, I throw myself down on my bed and pull out my phone. But I can't do it. As much as I hurt, I can't put myself back in the position of backing down or looking desperate. I made those mistakes with Paul and paid the price. Now, there's another price to pay as I think about Bret's question: am I willing to put up with the heartbreak of breaking up later? Do I want to drown in the shallow end or the deep end of the pool? I close my eyes and wait for one of us to blink.

26 / Bret

"Johanna, it's Bret. We need to talk," I say in the most serious voice I can summon.

She sighs, then maybe yawns. It is one in the morning.

"Did Sydney talk to you?" She says nothing, so I keep to my script. "I need to see you."

There's another pause until she says, "Bret, what do you want?"

"Come see me." I wait for her to hang up, but she doesn't. My sadness lifts.

"I can't drive up to Flint at one in the morning."

"You don't need to drive to Flint. I'm here."

"In Pontiac?" she asks. I can't tell from just two words if she's excited or angry.

"No, I'm at the Courtyard Marriott in Auburn Hills."

"I don't understand."

"I got it figured out."

"What did you figure out?" She now sounds engaged, not upset.

"How we can be together now, in the present."

"And how is that?"

I take a deep breath. "Let go of our past."

As I wait for Johanna, I do something I should've done a long time ago. I go through my contacts, and I delete not just Kylee's number but also her parents. I stop following her on Instagram and Twitter, then unfriend her on Facebook. I delete all of her photos on my phone and across my social media. My hand shakes as I delete the Radio Free Flint video from YouTube that showed her dancing.

About thirty minutes after my call, I get a text from Johanna. I pause before looking at it.

"Which room?" the text reads, and I breathe a sigh of relief.

"127."

About a minute later, there's a knock on the door. She stands outside, a vision wearing no make-up, a backwards baseball cap, and a long sleeve white t-shirt with worn blue jeans.

I let her inside without a word.

She walks past me and sits not on the bed as I had hoped, but in a chair. I follow her but stay standing. "So, you've got this figured out? Tell me how this works?"

I tell her about deleting Kylee from my life. I ask her to do the same with Paul.

"He's the one who keeps bothering me, not the other way around."

"What does he want?"

She looks down at the carpet. "I told you, Bret" she says. "Sex, maybe forgiveness."

"I guess he and I have one thing in common." She laughs and her eyes light up.

She rises from the chair and kisses me like we have been apart for years, not days. Weeks are all we have left, but it's enough. It is more than enough. It is all I need and want.

We kiss our way over to the bed. I sit down first, and she sits against me. I turn toward her and look into her eyes. There's something between us, even if it's only a beaten-up past and a sealed-off future. I peel off my shirt, then hers. We kiss and touch each other.

"Here's to no future," I say as I unbuckle her jeans

She pulls her jeans off, and they join her t-shirt on the floor. "And no past."

I pull a condom from my pants before I pull them down. She helps them off. We roll around on top of the sheets and disrobe until both of us have nothing left on but our socks.

"Here's to now," I whisper. "Here's to us."

27 / *Johanna*

"It is four in the morning!" mom yells at me, as if I didn't know. Bret wanted me to spend the night, but I knew that it would mean even more trouble. Looks like trouble found me anyway. It is only mom. After the confrontation with Paul, Dad's retreated from my life like he's ashamed he didn't do more to protect me even though that job rests solely on me.

I'm feeling almost high, so I don't need anything—or anyone—to bring me down.

"I know what time it is."

"Where have you been, Johanna?" Mom really needs more words in her vocabulary.

I put my hands on my hips and push my bottom lip out. "None of your business."

She looks desperate to light up a smoke, but her cigarettes are in the kitchen while she plays the stairway troll. "If you live under our roof, then—"

"Yes, I know. If I live under your roof, then I obey your rules. I know that, *mother*." I put as much of a nineteen-year-old girl's bad attitude into the word 'mother' as possible.

"Then I want you home at a decent hour," she snaps but doesn't move a muscle. I am not getting up those steps without getting into this fight. "I asked where you were?"

Two years ago, when I was with Paul, I almost answered that question with a lie. It is two years later, and I don't feel like lying anymore. I never liked being lied to, so why would I lie to her? "Do you really want to know?" I give her an out if only she'll take it.

She glances into the kitchen. "After that thing with Paul, I don't think there's anything you could say that would surprise me. I thought we raised you better."

"I asked if you really wanted to know."

"Who now? Another loser like Paul? Is it that Bret character?" Her tone knocks the wind out of me. "I want to know so your father and I can prepare for another scene like the other day."

I stand there with little head shakes. I roll up my fists in anger but don't say a word.

"You are so smart, Johanna. How do you make such dumb decisions about men?"

More head shakes, tighter fists. My tongue isn't tied, it's chained, so I don't say everything I want to say and blow her remaining illusions about my innocence down.

"Well, do you have anything to say?" She is a cartoon-snorting mad bull as she continues to rant about how immature I am for my age and how I don't know anything about life. This is the kind of verbal abuse I took from Paul; I'm better and stronger than that now. This ends now.

When she finally shuts up, I decide to wave the red flag, not the white one.

"I'm going to bed," I start toward the stairs. "I mean, I'm going to bed, again."

Mom looks like she hasn't slept while I am wide awake. Well, as wide awake as I can be after four hours of sleep and without any coffee in me. Dad is at work; Mom's trapped with her coffee, her cigarettes, and her rage. My closing words of last night hang heavy in the smokey air.

"Is it that weird Bret?" mom says as I pour myself a large cup of coffee in my Columbia to-go mug. I let the coffee—and the question—cool before I will answer. I owe her that much.

I stir in the cream and sugar before I answer, except she keeps talking.

"If you're going to be sleeping with this young man, then I think you should be able to tell your parents more about him. You didn't tell us anything about Paul and look where that got you. Since you can't make good decisions, we—"

I fight the urge to say fifty nasty things. "Yes, it is Bret."

"More white trash," mom mutters. She can slap my face from five feet away.

"You don't know anything about him." I know now is not a good time to mention that his dad is in jail for a DUI. "He's smart, funny, and he treats me nice."

"Unlike Paul," Mom says with venom in her voice.

I never told my parents the full extent of the verbal, emotional, and physical abuse I allowed Paul to pile on me, for it would just lead to a mom told you so moment.

"He's nothing like him. Well, other than his shoes."

"So, what are you and Flint boy going to do when you go back to Columbia?"

My engineer mom always knows the weak part of the Johanna machine. "I don't know." Bret talked of coming to New York, and I tried to talk him out of it. I told Sydney I didn't want to be alone this summer, which led me to Bret, but now I question everything. Not just because of last night, but because of the intensity of emotion we've shared in such a short time.

"You're not staying here to be with some white trash from Flint."

"Stop calling him that."

"I want to meet him again." She takes a deep drag, then expels the smoke rings I need to jump through to earn if not her approval, then at least her acceptance. "Tonight."

"I work until eight," I remind her.

"You seemed to have no problem last evening, I mean, this morning, getting together with him. Or what is it called now, 'hooking up'?"

I want to tell her it is more than that although that's the heart of it she doesn't need to know. Her honor society daughter really enjoys having sex. Better she not know that.

"I'll call him later."

"Now."

I know it is Saturday morning and why he is busy, so I put her off. "I'll call from work."

Mom takes another drag. She exhales and sighs at the same time. "How did you grow up so fast?" I don't say anything since it is a question I don't want to answer. Paul was like an emotional accelerator, and I can't help but keep my foot on the gas.

28 / Bret

"How are you holding up?" I ask dad during my now normal Saturday morning visit. Mom can't visit. Not won't but says she cannot. Cameron's a lost cause, and Robin is too ashamed or embarrassed or whatever it is that inflicts sixteen-year-old selfish girls.

"I'm working the AA program," dad says, looking dour and doubtful.

"That's good to hear." I want to ask him what made him stray from the path of the twelve steps, but it doesn't do any good to look back. And I don't think he'd tell me anyway, instead he talks about his AA meetings inside.

"I'm not going to fuck it up this time."

I don't know how to respond. I want to believe in my dad, but I always wanted him to believe in me. It wasn't a position we shared much during high school. I look at the clock on the wall. He catches me doing so. "You got some place better to be?"

I point to the drab yet scary surroundings. "And leave all this behind?"

"Are you still working?" he asks, almost like he assumes I'd quit or be fired.

I nod and fill him with boring details about my job.

"I'm still seeing that girl Johanna," I say to change the dreadfully dull subject of Goodwilling. "She lives down here in Pontiac. We actually met the day of your hearing."

"What is she in for?" He doesn't laugh when he says it. He assumes the worst.

"She was there with a friend." I answer since I can only suspect the reason: Paul.

I want him to say, 'So was I,' but that's not his style. We did the old-school standoff during most of my high school years until he broke me after I ran to him for help after Kylee broke my heart and then again when Hitchings broke my bones. But the breakthrough was fleeting. By the time I stood up for my school diploma, he had stumbled off the twelve steps.

"Is she a flake like that Kylee girl?" dad asks. Dad couldn't stand Kylee for who she was. Mom couldn't stand her for what she did to me. "Is she gonna wreck you like Kylee did?"

"Maybe. I don't know, and the fact is, I don't care." I learned in my summer before my senior year after Kylee's love and Hitchings' hate that I am resilient if anything. I wish dad would understand. I wish I could pass on that trait to him while he spends his time behind bars.

"Times up!" the guard yells. I reach to touch dad through the glass, but once again, he just hangs up the phone and leaves me hanging like a bastard son of an absent father.

I retrieve my cell phone from the locker when I return from the visiting area. There's a text from Johanna asking me to visit her house after her work. I think of the Edmunds, so inviting and enabling, but somehow, I sense that won't be the same vibe I get in Pontiac again, especially after Johanna's late arrival. My sense from what Johanna has told me is that her mom is the hanging judge and her father the executioner. There's only one way to get through this, which is some physical distraction before the event. I text back, asking the time. She says eight, so I ask her to leave work early so we can meet up at seven at the money draining Marriott to remind ourselves why we come together, literally.

We meet at the Marriott at seven, which only gives us an hour before we're due at her parent's house. She barely gets in the hotel room door when I start trying to get her clothes off. She is helpful in that endeavor. We've crossed the threshold from chemistry to connection.

"You want to come back over after the thing with your parents? I have the room for the night," I say as I let her push me against the wall so hard that the furniture in the room rattles.

"I can't risk it," Johanna says. "They've moved from neutral to negative."

We breathe heavily, yet still try to talk between kisses. "What did I do?"

Johanna unbuttons her blouse, then tosses it on the bed. "Well, this for a start."

"You told them?" I add my shirt to the growing clothing pile on the bed.

"Well, my mom's a pain in the ass, but she's not an idiot. I might have said something."

"Did they know about Paul?" She stops kissing me when I mention the stop word.

"No, but I wish they did. Maybe some loving parental advice would've helped then."

I laugh, then tug at her jeans. "Why are we talking?" I ask. "We only have an hour."

"Then you better shut up." And in a few seconds, she takes my words away.

29 / *Johanna*

Dad greets Bret at the door, only a half hour late as things got more involved at the Marriott than planned, not that dad needs to know it. I am sure mom told him about my bed comment the other night, but he's playing it cool with a hearty handshake and a welcome into the house.

"Johanna, you're late," mom says, making sure to belittle me in front of Bret.

"My fault, car problems." Bret lies, and that worries me.

Dad looks out the window. "Is that a Chevy?"

"What's left of one. It's more rust than a car at this point," Bret cracks.

Dad doesn't laugh and instead starts singing the praises of Chrysler.

Mom invites Bret to sit in the living room, relieved no doubt that Bret's not drenched in sweat and grease like Paul was the first time he visited the house.

Bret does his best to impress with stories of high school success, not mentioning Kylee once, and his job. Mom glares and shakes her head in disapproval at his Goodwill attire. Dad is not giving off any signals good or bad, probably just happy it is not Paul at his house again.

"And I do theater and I used to be in a band," Bret continues his good-impression parade.

Mom seems uninterested. "What do your parents do in Flint?" Twenty-question mom inquiries. Bret hesitates, then says "My dad's out of work, but my mom's working two jobs. "

I want this to stop. Bret doesn't deserve this interrogation. He's asked and answered everything and passed their inspection like some car down the assembly line. "We have to go."

Dad asks, "Where?"

I reply with my go-to one-word answer. "Out." Mom doesn't say a word.

Bret and I leave the house hand in hand, on our way to get skin-to-skin.

Bret doesn't even need to ask where "out" means since he never checked out at the Marriott. He's all Indy car racer once he hits the highway to get us back to the hotel.

"How long can you stay?" he asks when he parks the car.

I arch an eyebrow and don't say a word. Conversation isn't on the menu. Bret hurries out of the car, then opens the door for me. We walk hand-in-hand toward the room.

We're barely inside before we're all over each like we plan to never see each other again.

"Long enough," I whisper as we fall together into the inviting bed.

"Do you really have to go?" Bret asks as I start to get dressed.

I shoot him a sad smile. "My mom is—"

"No, not home tonight, but back to Columbia," he says softly, like sharing a secret.

"Bret, yes, I'm going back to school." I pull on the last of my clothes.

He climbs out of the bed with the sheet wrapped around his waist. "Could you at least consider staying? We're having such a good time. Why do you want to end it?"

"Bret, we can stay close after I go back to school. We can—"

"If you won't stay, then maybe I could move there," he says again, and I don't respond, which is like shouting 'no' without having to say the word. "Don't you want me there?"

"It doesn't have to be so black-and-white," I say. "We could make it work."

"It's not the same."

"We can stay in touch. You can come visit and—"

He turns his back to me. "Like I said, it's not the same. I couldn't do it."

"Do what? A long-distance relationship?" I ask.

"I just can't bring myself to trust someone again. If you'd ever been cheated on, you—"

"Would understand," I complete the sentence for him. "But Roman did cheat on me."

"There's a big difference. You didn't love him the way I loved Kylee."

Now it is my turn to laugh and not a gentle one either. "I think you are using the wrong verb tense." He says nothing and instead starts putting on his clothes.

"She is like a splinter in my eye that I can't get out."

"So, we can't have a long-distance relationship because you can't trust me because of her? Is that what you are saying? Kylee still not only controls your life but also mine?"

"She doesn't control my life, and you are one to talk with Paul back in your life!"

"So now we are getting into it!" I yell. He sits down on the bed and glares up at me.

"I guess we are!" Bret yells back then we just stare at each other like two gunfighters. This is not the relationship I want with Bret. I don't want the anger back in my life again.

"I guess I don't understand you and Kylee, just like you can't ever understand what Paul did to me that I can't let go of no matter how hard I try."

"So where are we?" Bret asks, and he gazes into my eyes. "You're not staying. I am not going. And after August, we're not staying together, so where are we anyway?"

I push Bret back on the bed, then crawl on top of him. "We're here, now."

30 / Bret

We're relaxing after having finished with another round of satisfying sex, which is something that Johanna mentioned that Paul never provided. After our brief fight, we talk about everything but the elephant in our lives: her soon-to-be departure for Columbia.

"Let's go. I can't stay out late again." We lie naked next to each other in the bed.

"What are they going to do to you?" I ask. My mom has not said a word about my early morning comings and goings. Having temporarily lost her husband to drinking, I think she's afraid of any confrontation that might push me away. Her acceptance is benign if not benevolent.

"Can I see you tomorrow?" I ask, knowing the clock is ticking.

She kisses me on the forehead. "Of course, Bret."

We make plans, get dressed, and then head out to my car. It cranks a couple of times before it starts, but soon, I find myself out on the highway with nothing but road in front of us, at least for another month, then I will hit a dead end when she moves back to New York.

I get to her driveway. We make out briefly in the car, encouraged by her and seemingly egged on by the switching on of a front porchlight and an opening of the front drapes. Our evening ends with a bittersweet taste on our tongues. After she climbs out, I turn on the music and get ready to start the long satisfying drive home. If tonight was somehow the last time we spent together, then my time with Johanna was totally worth it. I am happy for the first time in a long time. I turn to an Ann Arbor alternative music station with an eclectic mix from classic English punk to contemporary EDM and everything in between. I am in the zone of contentment.

I back out of the driveway and head up Eldridge Avenue. I get to the stoplight to turn on Rankin Road, but the car in front of me has slowed to a crawl, then a full stop. I honk even though my hearing is blocked by the blaring music from the car in front of me spilling out into the night. In a second, my eyesight is clear as I see the black Firebird parked in front of me.

It happens fast. The man—which has to be Paul since Johanna told me often about the black Firebird and I saw it in her driveway once—comes toward me. I quickly lock all the doors and get my phone ready to dial 911 although this far out in the burbs, and with all crime in the city, I doubt they can help me. Paul bangs on the driver's side window.

I'm just about to put the car in reverse while I hear louder sounds coming from the window. It is Paul kicking at it with his right foot. In seconds, the glass explodes, sending shards all over the front seats. I feel some of it cut the skin on my arms and face. I reach up and wipe away the blood. Paul reaches in his hand and hits the switch so the doors open, then he punches me hard in the jaw. Stunned by this blitz attack, I can't fight back. He pulls open the driver's side door, and in one swift motion, undoes my seat belt, then grabs me by the shirt. I try to fight back, but I am defenseless against his enraged onslaught. He's all fury, and I'm all fear. Fury wins.

He pulls me out of the car and tosses me on the hard pavement. The first kick comes right to the face. The next kick is to the ribs and knocks all the breath out of my body. "Are you going to fight like a man or just lay there?"

I think about Hitchings and the prom night carnage, except there's no Sean here to save my ass. I try to stand, but just earn another kick, this one to the face. Even though he's just wearing Chucks, the kick feels like he's got on steel-toed boots. I say the only thing I know to say when this happens, "Is that all you got!"

"You will leave her alone, you understand me!" Paul says enraged beyond belief.

"No!" I shout as I climb back up to my knees.

"I've beat up tougher women than you bitch!"

"You won't touch her again!" I shout back full of empty words and promises.

"And what are you going to do about it? Call the police. Big deal. What are they going to do? Slap my wrist again and send me to another worthless class."

I don't have any answers, so I take a mad desperate swing at his stomach, but it misses. My air swing is the last thing I remember.

I come to after I don't know how long. The Firebird is gone, and I'm stranded, bloodied, and disorientated. My ears ring, my head aches, and my extremities feel numb. I stagger to get to my feet, and the hot blood flows from my face, down my t-shirt, and onto my Chucks. The mix of red blood and my green Chucks makes me want to vomit, which I quickly do by the side of the road. I reach into my pocket for my keys and manage to pull the car to the side of the road, but I have double vision so I know I can't drive. I do my best to gather myself together and stumble down the road toward Johanna's house. Whatever good she might have still seen in Paul will vanish when she sees the damage he has inflicted. Slowly, step by stumbling step, I arrive at Johanna's. Exhausted, sore, and confused, I crawl up the front lawn like some guttersnipe. I bang on the bottom of the door, then fall face down. My blood trickles into the cracks on the porch steps.

31 / *Johanna*

"Oh my God, Bret, what happened to you!" I ask frantically after I open the front door to see Bret, bloodied and battered, face down on my porch. I help him stand, then he's bent over in a crouch. He doesn't need to say a word before I know the answer.

"Paul." Is all he says. I should be surprised, but I am not. I should have seen this coming and wonder what I could have done to prevent it.

"What's going on down there?" My mother yells from the top of the stairs.

"It's Bret. He's hurt."

I hear my mom start down the stairs. "What happened?" she asks.

I look at Bret, but yet I think of Paul and the image of him sitting in a jail cell, that Firebird free spirit crushed by four tiny walls. "He had an accident."

Bret doesn't react; he's too busy spilling blood from onto mom's white carpet. I help him into the kitchen and set him in a chair. I grab a towel and start wiping away the blood from his face. While I quickly clear it off his face, I see it dripping from his mouth.

"Bret, you're really hurt. We need to get you to the hospital," I say. By now, mom is on the scene. She quickly agrees and reaches for her phone. 911 I can only assume. That means explanations and consequences. "Don't bother, mom, I'll drive him."

"Are you sure?" mom asks. She looks concerned for Bret even if deep down she probably hates him for corrupting her not-as-innocent-as-she-thinks daughter.

"I got this." I'm in full editor-in-chief, take-charge mode. As the conversation swirls, Bret just sits at the table, moaning and holding his side. He tries to speak, but no words come out.

Mom flips me her car keys and then helps me get Bret onto her car. "You're sure?"

At the moment, I am sure of nothing other than my conflicted feelings, but I press on and do what is becoming my regular habit. I lie to my mother and repeat, "I got this."

On the way to the hospital, I call Sydney to meet me there. I need support. When I arrive, she's there with a worried look on her face, not one I am used to seeing. With her help, we get Bret into the emergency waiting room. It's her first look at him, and he's a mess.

"I need some help!" I cry out. At first, I am ignored in the chaos of the room. I go to the desk and tell my story, but the admitting nurse seems unmoved. She hands me a clipboard and a small novel of paper, but no entrance pass into the emergency room behind the doors. I fill out the forms, the words barely legible thanks to my shaking hand, and hand it back.

"It will be a few minutes," the lady says coldly. I return to find Bret hunched over with Sydney rubbing his back while wearing a concerned look on her make-up-free face.

"What happened to him?" Sydney asks, the concern in her voice evident.

I tell her the truth because it is understood that she'll keep my secret. "Paul."

Bret moves his arm up toward his mouth, then spits blood onto his shirt. "He ambushed me." Bret, through heavy breathing and busted-up jaw, tells us the tale. I feel my temperature rise with each word, and I grimace as images of Paul's attacks on me come into focus.

"You've got to do something, Johanna!" Sydney yells.

"It's just like before with him. I can't get out," I admit.

"He may never touch you again, but he's going to hurt you and those you care about."

I don't say a word because I have no vocabulary that matters. Sydney is right. I am wrong, but there's nothing I can do. I am helpless and hopeless. Paul has taken my power again.

"Maybe I should sue him," Bret mutters through his messed-up mouth. "It worked once, maybe it will work again."

Sydney gives me an odd look. "What is he talking about?"

I tell Sydney the story Bret told me about getting beat-up by a bully at his prom but then his father suing the guy's father and winning a civil action and judgment. "It is a fine plan, except Paul doesn't have anything to his name but a beat-up Firebird," I say.

"I'm sorry, Johanna," Bret says.

"No, I'm the one who is sorry. This is all my fault," I think about what Sydney said about taking responsibility as the only true path to forgiveness. "Can you forgive me?"

Bret reaches out, and I hold onto him, letting his red blood stain my blue t-shirt.

"Forgive you for what?" Bret asks.

"For dragging you into this mess, for not having my shit together, for all of this."

"Of course, I forgive you." Bret seems to be more coherent.

I feel a rush of emotion surge through me as I feel the burden of guilt lift. Maybe this is the one thing I could do to get Paul out of my life once and all for is forgive him. I could do it if he would ever accept responsibility.

"I don't want you to ever feel bad about anything on my account," Bret says.

I think of our talk in the hotel, about our relationship ending. I know that it will be a long time before I don't feel bad about the fact that we can't go on after summer is over. I project myself being alone in New York, being without Bret, and being lonely. It's not something I am looking forward to experiencing. Once again, I'll need to be strong like I need to be now.

"Bret Hendricks!" A voice calls out from the door by the emergency area entrance. With Sydney's assistance, I help Bret to his feet. A hospital worker pushes over a wheelchair, and all three of us set Bret gently in it. The hospital worker takes Bret back. I start to cry.

Sydney guides me back into the hard chair and puts her hands on my shoulders. "He's going to be alright." I nod even though she's a poet not a fortune teller.

"I know that," I say through tears.

"Then what's wrong?"

"I don't know what to do about Paul," I admit.

"He's got to pay for this," Sydney says forcefully, but I shake my head in the negative.

"I can't do it. It's too much. I will ask, even beg, for Bret not to press charges against Paul. I can't bear the thought of Paul's spirit stuffed in a small cell or my guilt of putting him there. He is the thorn in my paw, but I need to get free on my own to regain my power.

Sydney grabs my knee, hard. "Yes, it's too much you've let him get away with. Not just before, but this summer." She knows all about the scenes at my house and in the parking lot at work. I couldn't keep all of this hurt to myself.

"He's not to blame. That is all on me."

Sydney squeezes my knee harder. "That's bullshit, Jo. Complete bullshit."

"No, it's not. I put all of these wheels in motion. I stayed with Paul when I knew better back in high school. I let him back into my life this summer when I knew better. He's got his hooks in me, and I can't get free."

"What is it going to take for you to do something right? Don't you see that you've made all the wrong choices? How can you not see that as clearly as I can?"

I take her hand off my knee then clutch my stomach in as much emotional pain as Bret must be in physical pain. "See what?"

"That you're still in love with Paul."

32 / *Bret*

I come out of the ER not as bad as I imagined and not as damaged as I was from the Hitchings prom night annihilation. Nothing's broken—neither a rib or jaw—just a few teeth loose and a splitting headache from what the doctor says is a mild concussion.

"Bret, how are you?" Johanna asks. She looks worried like my mom used to look worried about me all the time. I guess I welcome their distress as a sign of caring.

"I need to get my car," I say. For some reason, all I can think about is my car stranded on the road and how I'll get home. I need to revive the mom empathy machine.

"No, you need to do something else first," Sydney says too loud.

"What's that?"

Sydney clutches Johanna's right hand, then says, "You need to call the police."

"Johanna?" I ask, but she is too busy piercing Sydney with her beautiful brown eyes.

"No, let me handle it," Johanna answers with grit in her voice

"That's the wrong approach," Sydney says, then points at me. "Look at him!"

"I said I'll handle it," Johanna repeats.

I'm too tired and hurt to argue. This Paul problem won't go away, but I think about my dad in his cell and wouldn't wish it upon anyone else, not even Paul after this attack. Part of a relationship is trusting the other person, and I need to trust that Johanna will do as she says.

"Can one of you drive me to my car?" I ask.

Johanna shakes her head. "You're not driving back to Flint tonight."

"Where will I stay? I'm fresh out of Marriott money."

"You can stay at my house on the sofa," Johanna says,

"How do you plan to explain that to your parents?" Sydney asks.

"I don't need to explain myself to anyone," Johanna answers, sounding strong and confident. Maybe I like her so much because I want to be like her in those ways.

I watch as Sydney glares at Johanna and know that whatever is going on between them is because of me and Paul. Paul and I are chained to each other even as total strangers.

"I'll get my car," Johanna says. Sydney nods in agreement, and they help me leave the hospital. It reminds me of the Hitchings' prom beating except I didn't provoke this. All I did was fall for Johanna. Even as my head throbs, I know it was worth it.

"Good morning, Bret," Johanna says. She offers me coffee, but I wave it away. My stomach feels like it is a roller coaster, and my head is still pounding. It feels like what I suspect a hangover feels like based on the mornings I've seen dad endure.

Johanna's all dressed up for work, which reminds me I need to call in sick to Goodwill. I don't think there's anyone to call to tell dad I won't be visiting this morning.

"How are you feeling?" It is Johanna's mother. She stands over me with a coffee cup in her left hand and a cigarette in her right. The smoke makes me want to gag.

"Ok, thanks." I kick into untruth-overdrive in front of all authority figures.

"That must have been some accident," her mom says.

I steal a glance at Johanna, but she adverts her eyes from me. "Hey, I guess so," is all I can think to say. I don't know what Johanna has told her mom, not just about why I am sleeping on their couch, but about our relationship at all. Do they like me because I make their daughter happy, or are they angry that she's wasting her summer with the likes of me? I don't know or care.

"Do you think you can drive?" Johanna asks.

"As long as I can stop at a bathroom to throw up, I should be fine now."

I look down at my clothes. My vintage Underdog t-shirt is stained with blood; so are my Chucks. My jeans are even more torn from when I hit the ground.

"Thanks for letting me stay here," I tell Johanna's mom. She forces a smile, then takes a drag on her cigarette. Johanna helps me off the sofa. I'm unsteady when I first stand up.

"I got this," Johanna says, which is her mom's cue to head back into the kitchen.

Johanna's smart, so I don't question her pronouncement.

"You're sure you can drive home?" she asks softly once her mom leaves the room.

"And you're sure you can handle Paul," I whisper in return.

"I made a mistake letting him back in my life even a little bit," Johanna says, "I've ended things with him before, and I can do it again. You need to trust me on this."

As if trusting others in a post-Kylee world came easy, so I merely shrug my shoulders.

Johanna grabs her keys, says a terse goodbye to her mother, and then we head out the door. It takes only a few minutes to get to where my car sits by the side of the road. I see specks of my blood on the pavement.

"Come up to Flint tonight," I say and touch Johanna's face gently.

"I can't do that. I need to stay here and keep everything together."

"But, Johanna, it is falling apart, and we know why."

She doesn't say the name, nor do I. It wasn't just his fist colliding with my face, but Johanna's past ramming into her present. And like the serenity prayer taped up in my dad's garage, I have the wisdom to know I can't change a thing. I hate it; I accept it; I move on.

33 / Johanna

I sit outside Paul's trailer, waiting for him to come home from wherever. I have steeled up my spine for this confrontation. I started this mess, so I must complete it.

I text with Sydney, who is all mad and mono-syllabic while I wait. I wonder if she's rethinking our plans to room together this fall because she thinks I'm wrong about Paul. Yet even as I wait for Paul, I find myself thinking about Bret and August when I leave for Columbia. I wonder how I got myself into that mess and how I will be able to get myself out of it. It will take an even more steely spine. Who knew matters of the heart were so hard?

As always, I hear Paul's Firebird before I see it. Fittingly, the song blasting is *"The Ties that Bind."* He's two years older, yet in the same house with the same car listening to the same music. I feel sorry and angry at him and at myself. I have not changed in two years, either.

I'm just about to get out of the car when I notice that Paul is not alone. There's a girl with him, and they are pressed up against each other. It kills me, but for a second, I am jealous. I arrogantly thought that I was the source of all his attention this summer even if all of it has been bad, but at least, he was paying attention to me again. How can I have a spine of steel when I am obviously a pathetic, immature schoolgirl without a brain in her head?

The screen door to the trailer opens, and Paul's mom appears. There's a brief shouting match between them before his mom retreats into the trailer. It looks like Paul is about to escape when I make my move. Maybe it is best he's not alone. This girl needs to be warned.

"Paul!" I yell out as I climb out of the Jeep.

"What do you want, Johanna?" His voice slashes me from the broken-up sidewalk.

"We need to talk." I steady my voice as I grow closer to him, as I pull away from his vice-like grip on my life.

"Not now." He dismisses with a hard stare as nasty as his cutting voice.

"Now." I fight right back.

Paul shakes his head, sighs, and slams his fist into his hand, just like he drove his fist into Bret's face. I can't let him walk away today with any thought he can hurt me or Bret again.

"Wait here," he tells the girl and then starts walking down the street. I follow. He's walking straight and sober under the bright afternoon sun. Unlike our last breakup, which took place one drunken night in the shadow of a mini-storage unit, this is out in the open. I feel safe.

I catch up with Paul and grab his shoulder. He spins around.

"What do you want?" His tone so hard and cold.

"Why did you attack Bret?"

"To protect you. He's no good for you, Johanna. You deserve better than some weirdo in a junked-up Metro. He's no hero."

"You mean like you?" I fire back.

He laughs. "I was good for you, Johanna. You were this shy little daddy's girl when I met you, when I let you kiss me, and now look at you. Don't tell me I wasn't good for you."

Paul is so clueless that I don't know how to argue with him, so I don't take the bait. Instead, I stay on task. "Paul, that was the last straw of last straws. My friend Sydney thought—"

"That fat chick you're always drinking coffee with?" He asks, then I realize that he's been watching me all summer like some stalker.

"She thought I should have you arrested for what you did to Paul. My father still thinks he should have called the police on you for that stunt you pulled at our house. I probably should have done something that night when you confronted me in the parking lot outside of work. I know I should get some sort of restraining order so you will leave me alone. I should—"

"Should, but won't."

Paul's not giving an inch. "Because I wanted you to get your shit together. I mean, I thought you were taking anger management classes. I thought you would learn how—"

"You know I was never very good in school." Paul laughs, so out of place and time.

"I'm here to tell you that it is not too late for any of those things. You can still change, but until you do, I want you to leave me alone. This is over, or else."

"You took my calls, so don't act like you didn't want this."

I don't deny him even though every fiber in my being knows better.

"Don't act like when we were together you didn't feel something."

I don't say a word in the present as he has thrust me into the past.

"And don't say you want me to leave you alone when you know you still want me."

I practice my right to remain silent in the face of these accusations.

"So don't come around here telling me what I'm going to do or not do. You'll do and say what I want. You know why, Johanna? Because you've not changed. You're older, but you're the same insecure, overweight girl that I turned into a woman two years ago. You're the same."

I try to summon righteous indignation, but all I feel is sympathy for Paul.

"Well, what do you have to say?" He challenges me. I came over to confront him, and he has instead taken control of the situation. I've again given over my power to him. No more.

"Nothing you say matters to me anymore," I say as harshly as I can, knowing it is now-or-never time. "I've told you what is going to happen. You are going to stay out of my life, or you're going to jail. I don't know the law, but I can't believe what you've done to me, and Bret isn't violating your probation for your threats against Allison. When you—"

Paul cuts me off with a laugh. "Allison? Who do you think is in the car?"

He laughs. I cry. He's right. Nothing has changed, so I just walk away.

I try to call Bret, but he doesn't pick up. Sydney is at work. I look in my contacts and decide since I am desperate that I need what they call in football a Hail Mary. I need someone who understands Paul better than I even do. I dial the number. He picks up.

"Brad, it is Johanna," I say cautiously. It's been some time since we communicated, but he is my last best chance to figure things out about Paul. If I can understand why he is the way he is then I can stay free. I need reason to trump emotion.

"Oh wow, how great to hear from you. How did your finals at Columbia go?"

I answer as quickly as possible and then ask him the same about Stanford. Once we get life details out of the way, I move on to what is really important. "Paul is back in my life, and I don't know what to do. I tell him to leave me alone, but he keeps showing up."

"He can be stubborn and persistent," Brad says. "Like he was with Vickie and Carla."

Vickie was the girl Paul really wanted, but he settled for me when she turned him down time and again. I learned later that she started to avoid him after he almost punched her.

"This is different," I say. "This is scary and dangerous."

"That's not the Paul I knew."

"You mean you really don't know about Paul and me?"

"Kara told me things, but Paul said they were not true. I didn't know who to believe."

"It was Kara who helped save me. She was the one who told me Paul was hurting Carla. She was the one who told me I had to end it because he wouldn't stop hurting me, ever."

"That wasn't the Paul I knew," Brad says. "He kept that part of his life hidden from me."

"Then, you must not have known him well. Let me tell you about your former best friend," I say, then unload my bruise-cruise on Brad from how Paul fucked with my head to how he bruised my arms and struck my face to how he broke my life. I start from the first push and end at the last punch. By the time I am done, I am crying tears that taste as bitter as black coffee.

Brad tries to console me with kind words, but everything is too harsh

"I don't know," Brad says. "His family life was fucked up with his dad running off and his mom running to Jesus. He was lost and left behind, which is bound to make anyone angry."

"But that doesn't explain why he would take it out on me. He said he loved me."

"He did love you – well, as best as someone like Paul could love someone. I have some distance from him now, and I guess that's good because I don't think I could be there for him like I promised I would." Brad sounds like he is hurting even if I am the one crying.

"And I can't be there for him now, either."

"So, he's alone again, and that's why he is lashing out," Brad says.

"Would you talk with him? He might listen to you," I plead.

There's nothing but long-distance silence on the line. "I can't do that."

"But we were friends too, Brad," I remind him. "Tell me something!"

"Just remember this," Brad says sounding all California cool. "Paul's a damaged little boy running around in men's clothing. Do you ignore a screaming kid who wants a cookie?"

"No, I guess you give them the cookie."

"Give him what he wants, then maybe he'll leave you alone."

I think of what Sydney said weeks ago, and I wonder if I can really give Paul the only thing I have left to offer him: forgiveness.

34 / Bret

As I wait in the hotel room for Johanna, I make yet another attempt to reach Alex. I've decided what I want to do as hard as it is: I need to leave Flint and go to New York. I want to stay with Johanna because I know I can't handle a long-distance relationship. I'll smooth things out with Alex and join his new band. I'll get a job in the daytime, gig in the evenings, and see Johanna every other waking hour that she has for me in her busy schedule. Two years ago, Kylee broke my life and my spirit, but I've come to reclaim it. "Bret Lives Again" indeed.

It takes ten tries, but finally Alex picks up, probably just to stop the phone from ringing.

"Hey, Alex, it is Bret, and I got some great news."

"I told you don't call me anymore. I'm blocking your number. Goodbye."

"Seriously, Alex, we've been friends for years, and this is how you treat me?"

"We were friends, Bret. Listen to the verb: were. I'm not in Flint anymore."

"Neither am I, for much longer. I'm moving there."

"What do you mean?" The tone isn't one of pleasant surprise but of irritated disbelief.

"I told you. I met this girl who goes to Columbia and come fall—"

"Don't come here for me. Like I said, we were friends. I've got a new life here, and you can't be part of it. I'm sorry that is how it has to be. I can't have one foot in Flint and one here. I'm all in with my music here, and I can't have anything, or anyone distract me from it."

"But it could be like old times. I could play bass and sing in your new band."

"I got a bass player, and I got a singer. Look, you're not welcome here."

"I'm not asking to move in with you, relax."

"I don't want you here." I feel my knees shake like twigs in a strong breeze.

From my dad to my old high school principal Mr. Morgan, I've never liked people telling me what I can and can't do. "Fine, I won't see you, but I'm moving there."

"Lose this number," Alex says, then hangs up on me. I think of a dozen questions I want to ask him about his attitude, but mostly just one: why are you treating me this way? I stood by Alex throughout high school. I stood up for him when Hitchings was putting the bad mouth on him at the prom. We laughed, giggled, and laughed some more, and yet, somehow, it all means nothing because I'm just some stupid kid from Flint who is part of his past. Fine, fuck him.

I'm in a bad mood until I get the text from Johanna. I give her the room number and wait. I'm still hurting, so I know of only one thing that will heal me. I touch the condoms in my front pocket, then turn down the sheet on the bed.

She knocks on the door. I let her in with a big smile, but she's in tears.

"Johanna, what's wrong?" I pull her close to me, but she pushes me away.

"Did I do something?" She walks past me and sits on one of the chairs. I sit on the bed to give her the distance it appears she wants, which makes me wonder why she made the trip.

"I spoke with Paul. I told him to stay out of my life."

"Is he going to do it?"

Johanna starts to cry louder now. "Yes, I think he is going to do it this time."

"You don't sound so sure." I stay anchored on the bed.

She looks at the carpet, then up at me. "I'm not sure of anything anymore."

"It's not too late. I could still call the police. The hospital has the X-rays and—"

"No, Bret, don't do that; I can't have him go to jail. I can't do that to him."

I drop my head as if Paul was hitting me again. I pause a long time before I speak the awful truth that I've known but denied all summer. "You are still in love with him, aren't you?"

"It's not love. It is more pity, but yes, I still have some feelings for him."

"Then what does this mean for us? I wanted you to come up here so we could be together, and I could tell you that I definitely want to come with you when you get back to school," I say.

"Oh, Bret, that's sweet, but—"

"But?"

"But I'm too messed up for you to invest your time in, let alone change your life around."

"You're not messed up. You're perfect."

She sighs and doesn't smile. "I'm not worth it. You trust me, don't you?"

I don't know what to think or say or feel or do or be. I have a concussion of the heart.

"I was right before. Let's just end this now."

My inside reels from the body blow. "So, you still think you are doing me a favor by breaking my heart?"

"No, that's not it. It's complicated. I didn't plan for us to happen."

"But we did happen, and you're here now, so what does that say?"

The tears increase as she speaks. "It says I made a mistake coming here tonight, but I wanted to tell you in person that I don't think we can see each other again. I love being with you, I love being in bed with you, but my feelings are all messed up, and I can't sort them out."

"Mine are clear."

"And mine are complicated, and that's the problem. You see the world as black-and-white, Bret, despite whatever color you dye your hair. But it is not that simple. I mean, I thought I was totally over Paul, and yet I let him back into my life. He caused havoc, yet I can't let him go. "

"You mean he can't let you go."

"You understand. Kylee? You know what I'm talking about."

"But she's not back in my life!"

Johanna rises from the chair and starts toward the bed. She says nothing until she stands right in front of me. "But what if she wanted back in, Bret, what would you do?"

I realize she has closed the distance, so she can read my body language and not just hear my answer. I face the inevitable: my addictive sexual attraction to Kylee. "We'd be in bed within minutes."

"We lied to each other and to ourselves." She brushes her hand against my face. It still hurts from Paul's attack, but nothing hurts more than her words. "We're both prisoners of our pasts, and we're not done serving time."

The air leaves my lungs, and I don't want it to come back. I can't think of a single word to say that will make things change. I'm screwed by a calendar I can't change and a past I can't forget. Time is my enemy.

She pulls my hand gently toward the bed, but I don't move my feet. Sex won't solve anything. We stare at each other as if there are more words, but we know she's said everything.

We share a bittersweet kiss, and then she's gone. From my room. From my sight. From my life.

I lie on the bed and pull out my phone. I keep the pictures so I can remember the good times but delete her number, so I don't try to recreate those good times or reach out to her like I did before when we broke-up the first time. I won't be Paul. I will let the past live where it belongs.

Even though I have the room for the evening, I can't stay because all of the sweet memories suddenly turn sour. I check out, get in my car, and head back to Flint in stone silence.

Once I'm in Flint, I will make no trip down memory lane or go down the alley to paint a new saying. There are no words to write because Bret isn't living; Bret is just numb.

35 / *Johanna*

I put away the contents of my last piece of luggage into the dorm room since Sydney arrives tomorrow, but I've been here for four days. I needed to get out of Pontiac as soon as possible, so I chose the early move-in date. After I broke up with Bret, I quit my job. I spent the last week in Pontiac in my room, eating ice cream and reading fantasy novels. I ran across my copy of *Howl* with Bret's contact information written in, so I threw it away. I didn't burn it like I did with Paul's stuff after he broke my heart in high school, but I didn't want the memory to linger of what I did to Bret. I hurt him, but it was the only right thing to do in the long run. Those last weeks would have just delayed the inevitable. It would have been more days of great sex, but it wasn't right. I still prefer to rip the bandage off the scab in one swift pull.

I greet people I knew from last year and introduce myself to new faces.

"Hey, Johanna, right?" I turn around and see a guy I recognize from my Journalism 101 class. "You living here this year?"

"David, right?" He nods, then smiles, a bright wide one. He's got dark brown hair and darker brown glasses. He's clean shaven and nicely dressed in a light blue polo shirt and neatly pressed Khakis. He's way too overdressed for move-in week. I'm in jeans and a faded blue Detroit Tigers t-shirt with my sweaty and now long hair covered with a red, white, and blue bandana.

"Hey, what are you doing right now?" David asks.

"Nothing." I somehow hope this is my answer for the entire term after the summer I had.

"Some of us are going out to hit the clubs and listen to some music."

I look away. "That's really not my thing."

"Look, where are you from?"

"Michigan" I don't bother to tell him Pontiac because no one's ever heard of it.

"Well, I'm from Minnesota. When I'm done at Columbia, I'll probably move back there, so I figure I should do as much as possible in New York while I can. How about it?"

"Ok, good point," I say. If I want to change, then I need to do different things. This is far outside my comfort zone, which makes it a perfect experiment for Johanna 2.0.

"That's great." He reaches out his hand, but mine stays by my side.

"Anything I need to bring?" I ask.

"Just your dancing shoes." He points at his feet. He's wearing green Chucks.

After dancing, David buys a pretzel from a sidewalk vendor after he calls us an Uber. He doesn't offer me a bite, which is fine since I'm worried about dorm food weight gain any way.

"You ready to start back to the grind?" he asks as we wait for our ride.

"More than ready," I say but don't tell him the reason. This summer, between the trauma with Paul and the drama with Bret, the academic rigor of Columbia should be easy. No exam choice will be as hard as the one I had to make breaking Bret's heart and my own.

"Me, too," David says, then starts talking too much about himself and what a writing rock star he is. I admire his confidence even if it comes off as cocky. I think about the journey I made from an insecure nerd to someone with more self-esteem. All it took was a trip to hell and back.

"Our ride's here!" David announces. He finishes the pretzel and throws the wrapper on the street. He opens the door for me and lets me get in the car first. He follows and leans in to kiss me. Before I can say no, his salty lips rub brush against mine. I gently push him away.

"What's wrong? Didn't you have a good time?" David asks.

"What does one thing have to do with the other?" I counter.

"I just really want to kiss you."

I want to say, "I don't want you to kiss me," but he wouldn't find it funny.

"Look, I remember you from last year and always had a little crush on you. Then you got involved with that grad student. I heard he cheated on you. I bet that's rough to get over."

"Don't remind me." I think how Roman never weighs on my conscience, and the only memory I have of him is finding him in bed with another girl. I guess I didn't care. I guess I still wasn't over hurting from Paul to feel pain again. I wonder how it really feels when it is someone you love, like when Bret found out that Kylee was cheating on him. I hurt thinking about it.

"So, what do you say, Johanna?" He moves closer, and I close my eyes. He kisses me and I don't think of Paul, but for a terrible second, I do think of Bret.

Bret who never calls or texts or emails or messages. Bret who turned the page this time without cutting his finger. Bret who I think of still when I'm alone at night.

"You okay?" David asks. I open my eyes to see this stranger across from me and regret the lover I left behind, not that I had any choice. Bret wasn't part of my future, but I welcome him as part of my past. "What are you thinking about?"

I can't answer David with another man's name, so I say nothing and let him kiss me again which makes me just miss Bret even more.

"So that's it," I tell Becca over breakfast at The Venus. I've told her the story of my summer since we barely saw each other after I got involved with Johanna. But now, I have time.

"I'm sorry, Bret," is all she has to say for about the past ten minutes.

"Can I ask you something? And I want you to be honest with me."

"I don't think I'm going to like the question," she laughs nervously.

"Why did we really breakup?" I ask. "I know you said it was because long-distance relationships don't work. What was it really?"

"Why do you need to know?"

"I'm not taking 'we're over' as an answer from Johanna," I say. I was fine for two weeks, but I've cried my tears, softened my negative thoughts, and hardened my resolve. "Unlike I did throughout most of high school with being bullied, I'm actually going to fight for something."

Becca sips her coffee, then picks at her omelet, until finally she says, "You're right. It wasn't just that. You obviously know that, right? I just said that not to hurt your feelings."

"I always figured you had a better reason than sixty miles between us."

"I wasn't your senior-year girlfriend. I was your rebound girlfriend," Becca says, sounding sad and wistful. "I was the cure for your post-Kylee blues."

I don't disagree with her. I just never thought she knew that ugly truth. She continues, "And I got that. I accepted that. I wanted a boyfriend to take me to my homecoming, prom, all of that senior-year shit, and you wanted someone to heal your heart, so we both got what we wanted." I reflect not on Kylee for once but on Johanna and the past months.

"I'm sorry if I wasted your time." I shake my head in disgust.

Becca laughs. "Bret, you were never a waste of time standing or lying down."

I blush.

"But when I was going away to school, I knew it was time to make a break. We could go our separate ways with no dramatic breakup or regrets. Best yet, we could come out of it as friends, talking like we are now. We couldn't have done that if we had some big blow-up."

"Somehow, I don't feel like I started over where you did," I admit.

"That's because you stayed here. Why, I don't know. Did you think Kylee would come back from college and find you here, then everything would be like it was before?"

"No." I answer, but I've always wondered if that was part of my decision to stay home.

"You can't live in the past, Bret." Becca, queen-of-the-obvious, states.

"That's why I want to go to New York with Johanna, to live in the present."

"But from what little you've told me, she's stuck in the past, too."

I push away my plate of half-eaten pancakes. "I don't want this food; I don't want this conversation. It is Johanna and only Johanna that I want. I wish I could convince her of that."

"You're not going to do that sitting at The Venus Coney Island in Flint, are you?"

I don't answer with my mouth, but my actions. I thank Becca again, wish her well in sophomore year at college, and then feel the car keys burning in my pocket. Before Becca's out the door, I've mapping the path on my phone from The Venus to Columbia. Like the great American poet Robert Frost wrote, I have miles to go before I sleep.

Seven hundred and sixteen miles to be exact.

37 / *Johanna*

The first morning of school goes well until my phone rings. It's mom.

"He showed up again late last night."

"Who?" I wonder which character from my past it is: Paul or Bret?

"Paul. He was drunk. He and your father got into it. He threw a punch, but he was so drunk that he barely touched your father. We called the police. They took him away."

I'm punched in the stomach, and I need to sit down on the grass in front of the student union where I was meeting David for lunch. I can't breathe, and my heart is racing. I've never had a panic attack, but I bet this is what one feels like. Paul has no one to protect him from his worst enemy: himself. "Johanna, you said you would handle this," mom says sharply.

"I thought I did. I told him what would happen if he got in my life again; I would see he was arrested. I thought I handled it by letting him destroy himself, as I knew he would."

"But you left that to us!"

"That was wrong. I'm sorry." I am near tears. Bitter, ugly tasting tears.

"And that's what he needs to say to you and to us except this time mean it," mom says.

"He apologizes for his behavior all of the time," I admit like an ugly secret.

"But it never changes, does it? So, what does the apology really mean?"

"Is he in jail now?"

"He's out until he pleads. Did you know about his violent temper?"

She doesn't know about all the things Paul did to me. The distance somehow makes it safe, so I finally tell her. On this bright, beautiful fall day, I finally tell my mother most of my secrets from my time with Paul. I can hear her suck in her breath, and it is not from the smoking but the shocking words coming out of my mouth. I talk about the good times, but I can tell from her reactions that it is only Paul's crimes against me that she wants to hear.

"Why didn't you tell us this?" She finally asks when I finish my painful tale.

"Because you would judge like you are now. Because you would think I couldn't handle myself. Because you would realize I wasn't perfect like you wanted me to be."

"We never wanted you to be perfect."

I pull myself off the ground and stand up for myself. "Yes, mom, you did, but Paul never expected that of me. He didn't expect anything from me. He just needed me to love him."

"Do you hear what you are saying? He needed you to love him. That's wrong."

"I know that now, but I got caught up in him, and I couldn't find a way to get out without you judging me, so I put up with it until it became too much. Until I realized he would never change, and because he didn't change, neither would I. I was trapped in a vicious circle."

"And you were obviously right," mom says all final. "So, what are you going to do?"

"Tell him to leave me alone, for the last time, this is over. Maybe it will take the prospect of going to jail to have that message sink in.

"But you said it was over?" Mom asks.

"I used the wrong penalty. I told him I would call the police, but he must have known that when he came over to the house that you would play that card."

"What's left to threaten him with?" mom asks.

"The only thing he really wants."

"And what is that?" mom fires back.

"My forgiveness. Even if you put him in jail, he'll come back out to terrorize us again unless I tell him that if he does, then I'll never forgive him."

38 / Bret

"Bret, my God, what are you doing here?" Sydney asks when she opens the door. "And by the way, you look like shit." With her unwashed hair and ugly blue pajamas, she's not one to talk.

"I drove straight through from Flint. Eleven hours and twelve cups of coffee."

"And how many bathroom breaks?"

"Not enough." I joke. "Is Johanna here?"

"She's out. Sydney gets this embarrassed look on her face. "Didn't you call her to let her know you drove eleven hours to see her?"

"I deleted her number," I admit. "But driving here was one of those grand, stupid, romantic gestures that my friend Becca told me not to do. I wanted her to be surprised."

"Oh, she'll be surprised, that's for sure." Sydney gives me a thumbs up, then laughs.

215

"When do you think she'll be home? Does she have class this late?' I look at my phone. It is ten thirty. She's not in class and Sydney is saying nothing. I feel like an idiot.

"Maybe by midnight she'll be home," Sydney answers.

"Can I crash until then? My back is killing me from the long drive."

"Sure, Bret, there's a small sofa in here. Come inside, please."

I walk past her. Papers, books, and soda bottles everywhere. I find the small sofa in the small living area, kick off my Chucks, and lie down. I close my eyes and have visions of Johanna falling from my mind. I deleted her number but couldn't delete her from my life.

I wake up when I hear the door open. It's Johanna. She's not alone. Some guy is with her. They are kissing in the doorway. I turn on the light.

Startled, Johanna breaks her embrace and turns around. "Bret!" she shouts but then whispers something to her lip-lock friend, and he vanishes into the night.

I rise up from the sofa. Sydney's door is closed. It's just the two of us.

"Why didn't you call first and let me know that—"

My post-Kylee jealousy drug kicks in. "Who was that?"

"Just some guy who lives in the dorm here."

"You're sure not lives in your bed?" I'm all shades of green and red.

"Like I said, he is just a guy I know."

I stand up and walk over to her. "Didn't take you long to get over me, did it?"

She shakes her head. "It's not like that."

"I'm gone out of your life for weeks and already—" I get closer.

"You never called, Bret. Or texted. Or anything." She moves back a step.

"I didn't think you wanted me in your life anymore. I gave you what you wanted."

"Don't say it like that!" She starts to cry for which I am to blame.

"Why, because it is true?" I reach out my hand to her. She doesn't take it.

"You're acting weird." She observes the obvious.

"Might have something to do with the eleven-hour drive, you think?"

"You drove all day to see me?" Her hand finally touches mine. Sparks fly.

"And I'd walk over hot coals if they stood between me and you."

"Bret, this wasn't a good idea."

"But this is," I lean in, my mouth against her just-kissed lips. I can probably taste the 'he's just some guy' on her lips, but I don't care. I don't care about anything but right now. I won't live in the past, and neither will she. Tonight is, again, about the here and the now.

We kiss for a long time standing then move over to the small sofa, but it's like those few times we made out in my car; there's not enough room for the passion and body parts we want to share. Finally, Johanna says the words, "Let's go to my room."

"What about Sydney in the room next door?" I ask.

Johanna laughs. "Don't worry. She's a sound sleeper."

39 / *Johanna*

I blow off classes as Bret and I spend the morning in bed together. We hear Sydney leave around noon and decide to spend most of the early afternoon in bed as well.

"I need a favor," Bret says as we emerge from between the sheets.

I hold onto him tighter than tight. "Name it."

"I want you to call Alex for me." I heard first-hand his hurt and anger over Alex unfriending him from his life. "He won't talk to me, but maybe he'll talk to you."

"What do you want me to tell him?" I ask.

"That I'm in town, and I want to see him, that's all."

I hesitate. "Do you think that is a good idea?"

"Why do you say that?" he asks.

"What did we say but failed to live up to? That the past was the past? Here's a chance to get it right and learn from our mistakes. We let our pasts ruin or rule us; don't do this."

He pauses and considers my words before he speaks, but says, "You're smart and I've always liked that about you. You are totally right, but it is a scab I need to pick."

"It's a mistake, Bret."

"At least I know that, unlike you."

I cover myself with the sheet and get out of bed. "Are you saying I was a mistake? You drove however many miles from Flint to New York to tell me this?"

"I didn't think you were a mistake, but you felt differently," Bret says.

"I wanted it over for all the reasons I told you, and I guess I needed to start fresh here," I say. "The past keeps dragging us down. I didn't want to get caught up again in something that was."

"But I could move here like I told you. It doesn't need to be a was."

"No, Bret, what we had this summer was wonderful, despite everything with Paul, but that's in the past." I think back to how I told Paul in the heat of our breakdown that he was part of my past, not part of my future. I feel the same now but won't say those cruel words because, unlike Paul, Bret never did anything to harm me. His only crime was bad timing.

"It will be wonderful again."

"It's not the same. My life is here now."

"And with some guy."

"His name is David, and he's none of your business.," I snap. I dealt with Paul's obsession and need to control me. I won't live through that again with Bret.

"I don't know what else to say." He sounds exhausted, and I feel nothing but guilty, not for leading him on or any of that, but because I can't give him what he wants: me.

"There's nothing more to say." I try to sound final yet fair and kind.

He sighs, then smiles, reaching his hands out to me. I fall into them out of habit and horniness. "Then let's use our mouths for something else," he whispers.

I'm about ready to kiss him when a dark thought comes over me. He is trying to control me just like Paul did except he's using sex rather than violence. I call him on it.

"It's not like that. I just really like to be with you, that's all."

"No. Whenever we had any issue, you used the sex to gain back control," I say. "You knew you had a hold on me, and you used it."

Bret laughs, but I'm not even cracking a smile. "You're one to talk."

"What do you mean by that?" I counter.

"You know. When I was in high school, I had this kid, Dave Hitchings, who bullied me."

"I know you told me about how be beat you up at prom and—"

"But it wasn't about violence with someone like Hitchings. It was about fear. If I was afraid of him then, he had power over me. I gave him my power, and I've done the same to you."

"Bret, you're wrong."

"It took me some time to realize that my real high school bully wasn't Hitchings, but Kylee," Bret says. Like every time he mentions that name, I want to scream "enough."

"So, you're the bully, Johanna," he says, but not in an angry tone.

"No, you are," I snap back

"So at least we know the score," Bret says. "But I guess I'm not a very good one."

I look at him puzzled. "Why do you say that?"

"Bullies get their way, and if I was a bully, then I'd be living here now, not just visiting."

I shake my head. "I don't want to go through this fight again."

"I didn't travel seven hundred miles for that," Bret says softly.

I raise my eyebrow, then smile. He smiles back. Two bullies, side by side. "Then what did you travel seven hundred miles for, Bret Hendricks?"

He just laughs, and we fall back into bed.

I have no success getting through to Alex much to Bret's disappointment. We go to a late dinner, and then, he suggests that we go to a club and dance. My last dance was at the senior prom with Marcus, but it is my junior year prom with Paul that I remember to this day in every detail. He had me emotionally and physically in his grasp, yet as we danced that night, I wanted to forget it all and spend the rest of my life with him no matter what. Deep down, every now and then, that feeling comes back to me like it did this summer to my deep regret.

"I got a great idea!" Bret says excitingly. "If Alex won't come to me, then I go to him. He says we're over. Well, that's hard to say in person."

"What are you talking about?"

Bret puts his phone to his mouth and says, "The Qwerty Club." He waits a second for the response, then he's all smiles. "He's got a gig with his band tonight in Brooklyn. I want you to meet Alex. He'll talk to me if I show up and catch him after the gig."

I think about how Bret and I did much more than talk when he showed up. For a second, I feel guilty, but it washes away from me. Bret knows even as we lie together where I stand.

But I know with one crucial difference: Bret wasn't an intense first loss with his hooks deep into my soul and my heart. He came along later and made my life better, happier, and more satisfying. I look upon my time with Paul with both a grin and grimace, but my time with Bret will only bring joy for knowing him and heartbreak for leaving him. Joy wins out with Bret.

40 / Bret

The small club is sparsely populated. The Qwerty Club is not only not the headliner, but they are due on first, so things in the music business are not really working out for Alex. We get a table near the front since it appears there's nobody else here just to see The Qwerty Club.

As we wait, I share with Johanna stories about Alex, Radio Free Flint, and all the trouble we used to get into for being salmon swimming up the Southwestern High School stream.

"I wish I would have met you then," Johanna says, "I mean, before Paul."

"And me before Kylee."

"We were only fifty miles apart, but it took a courthouse drama to bring us together."

"I guess something good can come from something bad."

The small crowd is stirring and restless for live music. I see the stack of The Qwerty Club CDs on a small, round table by the stage sitting quite untouched. On the tables are flyers listing upcoming The Qwerty Club dates. They seem to be making excellent drink coasters.

Finally, an MC comes out on stage. He cracks a couple of lame jokes to the uncaring audience, except me who appreciates them, but just causes Johanna to roll her eyes.

"Welcome The Qwerty Club!"

Alex and others come out on stage, looking more pop than punk. Alex counts it down, then the music starts, but there's no singer until a spotlight hits. She comes out. Her chestnut hair has a rainbow ribbon in it. Kylee kisses Alex on the cheek before she steps to the microphone.

I see them together on stage, and somehow, I know that it is not only a stage they share, but also a bed. It is the final coffin in my life as a nail who gets hammered the hardest.

41 / *Johanna*

I try to console Bret, but it does no good. Even under the swirling sounds, I hear him crying. I recognize Alex as the guitar player from Bret's band and the singer as Kylee, his ex. I can only imagine the amount of betrayal that Bret must feel again at Kylee's hands.

"Let's get outta here!" I shout at Bret while I glare at Kylee. I hate her on sight.

But Bret isn't moving. It is like he is frozen in place and time, not now, but back a few years when I know he considered Alex and Kylee the closest people in his life. Now this.

"Bret, you don't need this!" I pull at his arm, but he keeps staring at the stage. I am glad he is sober. I am glad he is not Paul. If so, he would be charging the stage in righteous anger.

"Now!" I shout, and it seems to wake him from his trance. He stumbles when he takes his first step away from the stage, but I help him walk through the club and out the door.

I step to the street corner and hail a taxi. Bret is still looking inside the club. When a taxi finally stops, I help usher Bret into it. He's more zombie than human at this point.

Once we get inside the taxi, he curls up against the side door, going full fetal. I try to hold him, but he just presses more up against the door. Realizing there is nothing that I can do or say, I simply stare out at the New York streets passing us by. A city of eight million people, but right now, I bet Bret feels all alone in the world.

We get to my dorm room in pretty good time for a New York Saturday night. I pay the driver and help escort Paul outside the taxi. The driver must think he is drunk or high, but only I know he is in emotional shock. I felt it when I learned that Paul had beaten up Carla, his last girlfriend before me. I felt it when I learned Paul had been lying to me about his drinking, and I felt it when I saw at my high school open house Paul's new girlfriend, Sarah, sporting a black eye.

When we get to the room, Sydney is awake, sitting at the front room table reading a book and taking notes. It is *On the Road* by Jack Kerouac, and I bet Bret would be impressed any other night but tonight. He would engage her in conversation, make her laugh, but tonight is not that night. Sydney looks up from her book but says not a word as Bret stumbles past her.

"Bret, can you speak?" I finally ask as we walk into my room.

"Alex and Kylee. I can't believe it."

I know there's nothing I can say, only something I can do. I lead Bret to my bed and for a little bit of time hope that I can take his mind off everything.

"I need to go back to Flint," Bret says as we wake up to the beautiful sunrise after an ugly night. He doesn't say why, and I don't ask him since we both know the answer.

"I know."

"Johanna, you meant so much to me," Bret says, "I'm sorry this had to end."

I hold back tears. "It's the right thing for both of us. We can't be together, not after last night. You're still hung up on Kylee. That's why you reacted the way you did, isn't it?"

Bret doesn't speak, letting his silence answer the question until he starts to cry.

"Don't cry, Bret " I say, and my words are magic as his tears cease. "We had a great summer. A summer we'll remember, but we won't let define us. A summer we learned a little bit about each other, but also some hard truths about ourselves."

"It started good, but things changed."

"And because we hadn't changed, it ends like this."

"No, like this," he says, then ends it with a sweet kiss of kindness and sweet memories.

42 / *Bret*

It's a good thing I have a day to recover before the next labor of my Herculean summer.

"Thanks for the ride," dad says as we walk out from the lobby of the Oakland County Jail. We've both done our time this summer. He's put on weight. I've lost some. I wonder if he's gained insight into his life like I have. I wonder if the same angry man who entered jail is leaving the same way.

"You want to get a big meal at The Venus when we get back to Flint?" I ask.

"No, I just want to get home to your sister and mother."

"They'll be happy to see you."

"Then why did they never visit?" He sounds sad, not angry in his question.

"It was just too hard for them to see you behind that barrier and in that uniform."

"But you were tough enough to do it. I'm proud of you, son."

"I guess," I say even though I didn't have a choice. Someone had to be the connection with my father, and strange as it may seem, somehow that was up to me, his prodigal son.

"I'm going to work the program again. As soon as I get home, I'm going back to the meetings. This time, it is going to stick, not like before. Not like last time."

I drive slowly because I need to concentrate not on the road but on my father's own journey from drunk to sober to drunk and I hope back to sober. I need to understand his path and his past. "So, dad, why did you start drinking again?" I ask knowing the full fear of asking why.

"It wasn't one thing. It doesn't work like that," he says slowly so I can take in every word. "It was a bunch of stuff building over time, and I couldn't keep it together."

"Dad, I'm sorry if any of my immature high school shit caused this to happen."

"Bret, I am the one who should apologize to you. That's one of the steps. It is something that a person has to do to make things right. I'm sorry I was so hard on you then and even when you came to visit. I'm sorry I wasn't a better father. I'm sorry I let you down by drinking again."

"I understand," I say, even knowing I can never truly understand another person.

"No, Bret, you are nineteen, so you couldn't possibly understand," he corrects me. "I had no job and no prospects. I had a wife who I fought with all the time and a son who hated me."

"I didn't hate you, dad. I thought you hated me."

"No man could hate his own son."

"But I do love you, Dad."

"And I need to earn that back. That's a personal step I am taking. I need to take what I learned in AA inside and apply it to the outside world with all of its temptations."

"Dad, it's going to be okay." I reassure him.

He sniffs and laughs, "Easy to say, hard to live."

"Don't I know it." I let slip during all this father-son bonding time.

"What are you talking about?"

I take my eyes off the road to look at Dad. He's gained years on his face, but I hope he's remembered the night we finally connected after Kylee cheated on me with Sean. I need him again to be there for me even if he's not the strong presence I once feared and loathed.

"It is about that girl Johanna," I begin, and I spend most of the drive from Pontiac to Flint telling him the good, the bad, and the ugly. I leave out the great sex.

"You sound pretty beat up," he says when I've run out of road and pull off on the 12th Street exit. I wish I could show the "Bret Lives Again" writing, but I don't believe in it.

"It gets worse," I say, then tell him about Alex betraying me with Kylee. He cut me out of his life because of her. Two years later, and her actions still shake me.

Johanna was right. I was still chained to my past and unable to fully, emotionally, connect in the present.

"We've both had it rough," dad says, then wraps his arm around my shoulder. "And we both survived, and maybe with what we learned, things will get better."

"Things will get better," I repeat. He pulls me closer, so it makes it hard to drive.

"It's all about the serenity prayer," Dad says. "God, grant me the serenity to accept the things I cannot change, Courage to change the things I can, and wisdom to know the difference."

I think about Kylee, then Johanna, and know they are things I cannot change.

"You know what I would like to change, other than my quitting drinking?" Dad asks.

"What's that?" I ask.

"This relationship between you and me, son, between you and me."

I almost drive off the road at the kindness of these words, but instead, I press on toward home. The journey goes quickly with dad doing most of the talking, running through the twelve steps, but I think about the two big steps I made this summer: one away from Kylee, one toward Johanna. One haunted me, while one made me happy. I choose happy.

43 / *Johanna*

"My roommate isn't home," David whispers as we walk by his dorm room. We're both damp from our energetic dancing and the evening drizzle. I guess because I can never slow dance again without thinking of Paul. "He's down in Jersey, visiting his family."

I stand on the threshold. His hand is on my waist. I brush it aside.

"What's wrong?" David asks as he moves his hand up my shoulder.

"Not tonight." I let him kiss me before, so he is back for more.

"Why not?" I don't think of a hundred reasons, just Paul and Bret. Paul for what that emotional attachment did to me and for the sexual hold Bret had on me. I need to be free.

"Too soon." I respond and gently push him away, but he doesn't budge an inch.

He licks his tongue on my neck. I recoil.

"It's never too soon." He goes for my neck again. I push him away harder.

"What's wrong with you?" he asks through gritted teeth.

I know there is only one right answer. "Nothing."

David grabs my hands and tries to pull me inside his room, but my feet are in concrete. "I thought that we—"

"You thought wrong."

"No, you're thinking wrong. All of you small-town girls are such prudes."

If only he knew, but he won't because it is time things changed.

"I'm leaving now." I break away from his grip and start back toward my room. How much easier it is to end something before it begins. Falling back into another relationship too soon is likely to end in another crushing disappointment. Until I get a better handle on myself, I can't make a real connection with another person. I need to be strong enough to be alone, just like I was strong enough to get out from under Paul's control of my life and Bret's connection to my heart.

Sydney is still awake when I get to the room. She's rereading *Howl,* and I regret throwing away Bret's copy, but not Bret's passion. I'm slowly coming to realize that your past is something you take with you with every step you take, but you can't let it control your path.

I tell Sydney about David, and she doesn't act surprised. "These college boys. They're all alike." I think how different, in ways good and bad, that Paul and Bret were.

"He seemed nice enough, but you just never know," I admit. "But he is pushy and controlling. I don't need it again."

"You can do that to yourself, Jo."

"What are you talking about?" I pull up a chair next to her.

"Focusing on Paul again. You can't live in the past. You can't let it control you."

"I don't." I protest, but Sydney laughs. I am reduced to tears because I know she's right.

"You can't forget, Jo, what you can't forgive." There's a rainstorm outside, but it's as if I've been struck by lightning. It is like the time Kara asked me, after seeing the bruises Paul left on my arm, if I planned to wear long sleeves all my life. Sometimes, it takes another person to tell you the truth right in front of you that you cannot see. Forget and forgive must go together.

I get up, stagger into my room, shut the door and open the window. Outside, the noise is loud from the city streets, but inside, all I hear is the beating of my heart. I pull myself together.

I take out my phone. I dial the number, and Bret answers.

Before he speaks, I say the magic words to break the curse, "Bret, can you forgive me?"

"For what?"

"For leaving you, for letting you down, for everything."

There's silence on the phone. I wonder if his dad is home. I wonder if he's happy. I wonder if he still thinks about me. I wonder, but I don't ask, I tell. "Bret, please forgive me."

He talks in circles, but I drive to the center that cannot hold. "If you don't forgive me, then neither of us can let go of this past." I fail to hold back tears that match the rain outside.

"Why would I want to forget any of it, even you, breaking my heart?"

"You don't need to forget it, Bret. We can't let it define us. We've both made that mistake. Let's learn from it. Let Bret live again without my words on the wall covering you up."

"You were not a mistake." Bret is crying too.

"Forgive Kylee, forgive me, forgive yourself," I beg. "Say you forgive me."

More silence, more tears, then he releases me, saying, "Johanna, I forgive you."

"Thank you, Bret, thank you." I hang up the phone, pull in my tears, then take a deep breath. I cradle the phone in my hand and look out at the trees casting shadows from the streetlights on the sidewalk. I need to live without shadows. I take the star necklace off and do what I should have done a long time ago with Paul's final gift to me. I pitch it in the trash, not out of rage but resignation and relief. I dial the number to put an end to it once and for all.

"Paul, it's Johanna."

44 / Bret

"Johanna, I forgive you," I say, not out of anger, but kindness and understanding. I forgave Kylee from the wrongs she did to me, so it is only right I do the same for Johanna who did nothing to me except break my heart, not that we both didn't understand that would happen. That's the risk you run with romantic relationships. It's a risk worth taking again and again.

"Thank you, Bret, thank you," she says and then hangs up the phone. It sounds like she's crying. I hope someone—maybe even David—is there to clear away her tears with a tender kiss.

I wonder if it will be the last time that I will speak with her. Was it a summer thing or was there something more there? Was it just sex or a real human connection? I'll know, I guess, in a day or two if we communicate in some way even if our last words and kiss said everything.

And everything I could ever think about Kylee has been asked and answered. The corner of my heart that cared for her died when I saw her kiss Alex on stage. It died for him, too. They owe nothing to me, and I guess I wish them happiness although part of me wants to warn Alex that he has just entered the eye of the human hurricane named Kylee Edmonds.

I look at the time. It is past midnight, and for the first time in some time, I'm happy that I still live in Flint because I know that Meijer is open twenty-four seven. I grab my keys and head for the garage. Dad is there, still awake, and sipping something from a white coffee cup. I don't say a word and I don't judge; those are twelve steps he needs to take on his own. I hope, like me, like Johanna, and unlike Paul, that he has the courage to change.

At Meijer, I head immediately to the hardware section. No one questions why this ludicrous looking near twenty-year-old is buying a gallon of green paint and a roller at one in the morning. I'm sure the clerks have all seen stranger things than this purchase.

I head from Meijer down Hill, over to Fenton, and down to 12th street. I turn into the alley just as a train rumbles by on the nearby tracks. My car vibrates along with my heart.

I am quite alone, in every sense of the word as I stare at the graffiti-filled wall.

Somewhere beneath it all, I once painted in "Bret Lives Kylee." But when this proved to be false, I used a hammer to chip away her name, so it read "Bret Lives," then this summer, "Bret Lives Again." The years of hurt and heartache call for another message to fit my current life and times.

I stand before the wall like I suppose an artist does with his or her canvas except I don't need inspiration to pull from to create. I have bitter Kylee and beautiful Johanna experience. I feel like I covered some hard miles on this human highway but came out a better person because of Johanna. I forgave her, and I feel no guilt or regret or anger. My numbness has vanished.

I take the paint from the car trunk. I leave the car running and kick out not Radio Free Flint jams, but classic Clash, "Death or Glory" from *London Calling*. With the Clash bashing in the background, I start the work to reclaim my present and my future by putting an end to the past. I risk retaliation when I cover up the gang graffiti to mark this territory for Bret, but tonight, I have no fear. I am nothing but heart and soul. Death or glory, this is not just another story.

I paint over the wall as I keep the epic "Death or Glory" on replay. Slowly and with a steady hand, I paint the only message that matters: no past and no future, just present tense.

Bret is.

Patrick Jones is the author of over fifty books for young people, both fiction and nonfiction, most recently *Clicked* and *Teen Incarceration: From Cell Bars to Ankle Bracelets*. Jones has presented training workshops for teachers and libraries in all fifty states and made hundreds of school visits.

He can be found at www.connectingya.com and https://www.facebook.com/Patrick-Jones-24920877092

www.ingramcontent.com/pod-product-compliance
Lightning Source LLC
Chambersburg PA
CBHW010346220726
48290CB00016B/2651